A Question Of Murder

A QUESTION OF MURDER

Mystery Beckons Astrid

Camille Mariani

A QUESTION OF MURDER
MYSTERY BECKONS ASTRID

iUniverse books may be ordered through booksellers or by contacting:

iUniverse
1663 Liberty Drive
Bloomington, IN 47403
www.iuniverse.com
1-800-Authors (1-800-288-4677)

Because of the dynamic nature of the Internet, any web addresses or links contained in this book may have changed since publication and may no longer be valid. The views expressed in this work are solely those of the author and do not necessarily reflect the views of the publisher, and the publisher hereby disclaims any responsibility for them.

Any people depicted in stock imagery provided by Thinkstock are models, and such images are being used for illustrative purposes only. Certain stock imagery © Thinkstock.

ISBN: 978-1-4917-9748-8 (sc)
ISBN: 978-1-4917-9749-5 (e)

Print information available on the last page.

iUniverse rev. date: 05/18/2016

Also by Camille Mariani

Lucille's Lie
Aletha's Will
Pandora's Hope
Links To Death
Invitation To Die
Prelude To Murder
Astrid's Place
Abram's Puzzle
Aura Of Peril
Justice, Right Or Wrong

To Mary Thomson, my long-time friend across the sea

It is a mistake to look too far ahead. The chain of destiny can only be grasped one link at a time.

--*Sir Winston Churchill*

PROLOGUE

＋＋＋＋＋＋

May 1, 1945

A German invasion was imminent. That was the word along coastal Maine, south of Twin Ports, as rumors of a lurking German submarine circulated during the final days of World War II. After the war in Europe officially ended on May 8, many wondered aloud why a German U-boat would comb the U.S. east coast just before surrender; but, at the time, more than one person claimed to have seen such a boat. Some had no doubt that they saw foreign-looking men lurking around their properties. No question they were from that U-boat.

A housewife swore that a man she saw was a German spy sneaking along the shore like a treasure hunter, darting into the woods and back to the water again. She kept her children in the house for three days until they tested her nerves to the breaking point and she sent them outside with specific instruction not to go to the shore.

A fisherman boasted that he watched through binoculars while a foreigner made his way down the beach. Who but an enemy up to no good would hide behind a big oak tree when a couple of teenagers walked hand-in-hand down the lane to the shore? By the time local members of the Home Guard could be summoned, the foreigner had disappeared.

Digging clams, an old man saw someone watching him from the embankment above the shoreline. He stood up, and the stranger retreated into the woods along the hillside, just disappeared from sight. Being far out on the clam flats, the old man decided not to pursue for fear of being shot. And, oh yes, he was German all right, dressed in a sailor suit that didn't look like one of ours. No American sailor would run from him, anyway.

As she took clothes off the line behind her house, a woman looked down the open field to the beach and saw a man in white sailor uniform observing her. Of course it was a German spy, she said, you could tell by his spooky looks. She ran into her house and locked the door. When she peeked out her window, he was gone.

And so rumors persisted, tensions built, neighbors gathered at general stores and talked in hushed tones about the probable invasion. Local men who were classified 4-F, farmers, fishermen, or those too old to be called up for service, repeated stories about what they saw. They planned signals, devised hideaways for the women and children, prepared traps. No enemy would take over their homes and lands or harm their families. They were ready to fight with pitchforks, axes, rakes, scythes, hunting guns--whatever they could find that would strike a deadly blow.

While fears, imaginations, and plans grew, speculation sparked most of the discussions. But no one knew the truth—that a German U-boat really was cruising along the Atlantic seaboard, including the Gulf of Maine. Scouts were, indeed, sent ashore. And among the spies, one had no desire to return to Germany. Locals would have been even more unsettled had they known what that lone sailor was up to. On this first day of May, after months of preparation, the seaman slipped off the *unterseeboot* when, under cover of black storm clouds, it surfaced at night to begin its exit from the Maine coast to the vast Atlantic open sea headed for its home port.

Karl Ludwig believed he would not be missed right away, so he didn't worry that a search party might come after him. He planned to hide until the war ended and then seek mercy so that he might become a U.S. citizen. He had no idea that his future could be as bleak in the land of the free as it would be in his homeland. His desperation drove him to dream that there would be a better life for anyone who denounced Nazi terrorism.

He threw off his heavy jacket, tied his shoes together and secured them around his waist before jumping into the water. Even so, his clothes felt like lead weights once in the water. He couldn't have chosen a better time to abandon the boat than this dark night, but he had not expected his energy to be tested to the limit so quickly. The frigid water, wet clothing, and now a sudden squall sapped his strength, trapped him in his own folly. What if he couldn't get to land? He did not want to drown. He had been sure he was prepared to swim ten miles if he needed to, but this was less than half that distance. It was rough, squally and nothing like what he anticipated. The weaker he became, the more he had to remind himself to keep going, keep the arms and legs moving, head up. Choppy waves slapped his face, forced water down his throat. He spat brine on every stroke, and still swallowed the foul stuff. *Don't give up,* he thought over and over, but his mind finally began to drift. He could feel nothing. He couldn't lift his numb arms any more. It was no use. He'd have to relax and drown.

He raised his head. And he saw it. Land! He was right on target. It wasn't too far. *You can do it. Roll over, tread water.* On the roll to his back he saw a flash of light behind him. He listened but could hear nothing over the rumbling waves and roaring wind. Not possible that it was a raft, not possible that he had been seen going overboard. He kicked at the waves and moved on inch by inch.

At last, gasping for breath, he crawled like a baby on hands and knees out of the water and onto a beach. This was not the mainland. On a map he had chosen this island, called Twilight Isle, because it appeared to have woods and no bridge to the mainland, yet it was long. With any luck, he could hide out in the woods and forage for food at night, if he didn't die of hypothermia first.

He was here! He'd planned his freedom long before boarding the U-boat. He swam almost daily in cold waters, studied U.S. maps, and constantly recited to himself what he knew of English. Except for the language, he felt ready. How he would survive was still a question, but it didn't matter. If he should be caught and imprisoned, he would tell what little he knew and ask for political asylum.

Now he lay reeling, choking, retching, shaking on this little patch of island sand, his confidence as weak as his body. This was a foreign land where people were his avowed enemies. He couldn't expect to be welcome. But he hated the war and abhorred killing. In the confines of the U-boat he felt like a sardine packed in oil and grease, breathing rank air saturated with odors of dirty feet, sweat and smoke, eating food that tasted like diesel fuel. He had no privacy. Baths were salt water wash-ups. How many times he felt like screaming and running from that prison, with no place to go...not until they reached this particular bay.

He would miss his comrades and his homeland. But go back? He remembered the day that two of his closest friends were shot for their defeatism in the face of a lost war. He had to hold his breath to keep from becoming sick. He might have been one of them facing the firing squad if he hadn't been able to hide his discouragement, if he had repeated what others had been saying for several months—that the war was lost. It was whispered, and he didn't doubt it, that some 20,000 were court-martialed and executed for expressing disillusionment with Hitler's vision of Germania. When his own crippled grandmother was carted away like so much garbage, no doubt to her death, he decided he would escape the horror and the abuse of innocents one way or another.

He looked out over the roiling black water in the direction of his recent home, that narrow, stifling, steel jail, on its way back home as ordered. The months of preparing for this moment now seemed like mere fantasy. He was miserable, more alone and lost than he'd ever felt in his life. What had he done? His homeland was lost to him forever. Here, he might be shot if discovered. If he were sent back to Germany, definitely he would be shot as a deserter.

He had no choice. Must go on. Find a warm place to calm down and plan the next move. He needed food, water, and dry clothes. Somehow he had to rest as well. Standing up, he studied the terrain behind him and saw a mammoth house set back from the cliff. It appeared to be dark inside, though there could be lights behind blackout drapes. Or it could be vacant.

Even if someone should be in it, he could probably hide in the cellar. Maybe there would be preserves to eat. He staggered toward the embankment, prepared to claw his way upward, only to find a long set of wood stairs. On worn boards that threatened to break under his weight, he managed to reach the top, painful step after painful step. He fell on the grass to rest before going on. Moonlight flashed on and off like a dying incandescent bulb, as racing clouds began to disperse, giving him moments to study the surroundings. When the moon went behind clouds again, he stood on wobbly legs, lurched and tripped along the back lawn to the house. Now he faced more stairs.

Never mind the cellar door below the staircase. Go up and avoid a dank, musty area all too much like the boat. His heart beat so fast that he feared he might pass out. Gripping the stair rail, he waited to calm down. Be quiet. Don't alert anyone if they're upstairs.

Finally ready, he took his dripping shoes from his waist, drained them, and slung them, still tied together, over his left arm. At the top he walked across a wide porch and tried to peek through a half window in the door. Only darkness. Of course, another blackout shade. He tried turning the knob, surprised when it turned easily and noiselessly. He walked inside, and carefully closed the door. Leaning against it, he listened but heard nothing except the tick-tick of a grandfather clock from another room and his own uneven breathing.

His eyes began to adjust to the dark kitchen. Now he could feel his way along a counter to explore the cupboards for food. Taking one step, he jumped back when a bright light flashed in his eyes.

"Who are you? What are you doing in my house?"

A woman's voice. He raised his arms high. The shoes clunked to the floor. The only word he could think to say was, "Asyl. Asyl."

That's wrong. How is it said in English?

"You're asking for asylum?" the woman said in perfect Deutsch. "You want me to give you sanctuary?"

"Spiechen sie Deutsch?"

She didn't reply, so he continued, hoping to convince her that he would not hurt her.

"I defected. No weapon. No harm. I left *hous und hof* forever to live free in this country. What will they do to me here? I need help. Please help me. I can't go back to that torment. I will work for you."

Still silence.

He tried in English, slowly, "The war…is…needless…killing."

The overhead light came on. He blinked. A stately woman with clear blue eyes and a mantle of dark hair pointed a small handgun at him with one hand. She held a flashlight in the other. A floor-length blue robe, drawn tightly around her, emphasized a slim, firm body.

He fell to his knees, clasped his hands, as if in prayer. He could read nothing in her stern expression, whether she believed him or whether she intended to shoot him. She must believe him. He had come this far. There was no going back.

"Please. I beg. Please help me. I come in peace."

"I'll get you something to eat, and you can tell me why I should aid and abet the enemy. First, you'd better get into something dry. I'll point the way and you walk ahead of me, up the stairs. There are men's clothes in one of the rooms. There's a bathroom next to it. Wash off some of that stink. When you're ready you can eat and tell me why you are here and why I shouldn't call authorities to pick you up."

Obviously a tough woman, she couldn't be more than 25, his own age. He was sure she would shoot him as easily as she would swat a fly. He needed to gain her trust if he wanted help. He hoped he had found a sympathetic person.

Over his shoulder he said, "I am Eddie Smith."

"If you say so," she said.

She directed him to a room and he went to the bathroom, stripped and poured hot water into the basin. As much as he longed to get into the bathtub, there wasn't time to soak in it. He held his hands in the water for a long few minutes to regain feeling. They began to ache, but he didn't care. He'd be clean for a change. He wiped himself as he went to the bedroom where he found clothing in drawers and the closet. He avoided taking any of the better clothes, but chose dungarees, a cotton shirt, and a pair of well-worn shoes, and left the room. She was still waiting outside the door.

"Good," she said. "I couldn't tell if my father's clothes would fit you, but it appears they do."

"*Danka*. What shall I do with my clothes? I put them in the tub."

"Leave them for now. Come downstairs."

She prepared scrambled eggs, toast with strawberry jam, and hot chocolate, a tasty meal after the dried, sometimes spoiled food he ate on the boat. They talked while he ate. He told her about his decision to leave the German service and seek asylum in the United States, then how he had gone about the plan and waited for the exact moment to escape the U-boat. He said he was sure the war would soon be ended. She appeared convinced that he was telling the truth.

"Did you not have a plan for what you would do after getting off the boat and coming ashore?" she asked.

At that moment, the door flew open and a uniformed German stomped into the kitchen. So, they did send someone to search for him. How could he have been found like this? The upstairs window. It must have been uncovered, making the place a veritable lighthouse. He hadn't noticed.

"He comes with me," his comrade shouted. He pointed his rifle at the woman.

"No!" Karl knocked over a chair in his haste to stand in front of her. "Do not shoot her. She is a good woman."

"Where is your uniform? Get it. You will come with me."

Saying nothing, the woman nudged Karl aside, turned to face the gunman, and shot him through the pocket of her robe.

Surprised and dumbfounded, Karl stared first at the body and then at her. It could have been his body on the floor had she chosen to shoot when he opened that same door. His hopes for her help rose…and then quickly fell when she turned the gun toward him.

CHAPTER 1

Saturday, July 4, 1992

Abram stood beside the dresser watching his wife waste time on a gorgeous Saturday afternoon when they should be at the Fairchance College Fourth of July fair. He missed it last year when he had to work, but now it was time to enjoy sunshine, fresh air, and the fair for a good old celebration complete with greasy fried foods and homemade ice cream. Not but what he appreciated the inside activity right here. He suppressed a smile when he thought how like a snake Astrid moved, all curvy and supple. Undoubtedly she would not be inclined to view that as a compliment and he might just possibly need to duck a flying object if he said what he thought. She did have a bit of temper now and then.

He recalled when he met Astrid at her front door and how he admired this blond, lanky Swede with three outstanding features, one of which was her deep voice. He was bowled over on the spot. At the time he thought she was a working woman who couldn't afford to have him upgrade that old house. She was working, all right, but thanks to her wealthy grandfather, had enough money to rest on her pretty tush forever and make over a dozen homes.

"I know you're here, but I'd swear you've gone somewhere else," she said. "What has you in such deep thought?"

"You, of course."

He watched her reaction with amusement. She had a cute way of wrinkling her nose at him, normally followed by a quick kiss. She didn't disappoint him now. He often wondered how he got so lucky, finding this rare individual to live with the rest of his life.

"So tell me," he said. "Why are you packing today? We don't leave for three days."

Astrid continued to fold and neatly pack. Her loud sigh said how moronic the question was. Abram knew why she was packing now. She had told him a dozen times. It would be a busy weekend at *The Bugle* with all the Fourth of July activities: the college fair, a parade, the grand opening of the new pet store, fireworks in the park, and who-knew-what. They'd have less than two days to get the newspaper ready for deadline Tuesday noon.

"Who are these people anyway?" he asked. "I don't remember meeting them."

"They were at the wedding last year. Helena and Eddie Reese. She's Marvin's aunt. I guess they've traveled everywhere in the world and speak several languages. They got back just in time for Marvin and Dee's wedding and have remained in the States since then. They decided to retire to their home in New York, and to come to their cottage on Twilight Isle summers, according to Dee."

"I didn't meet them."

"You did."

"No, I didn't."

She held up a white sweater and studied it before folding and packing it.

"They were that older, handsome couple, maybe in their late sixties or early seventies. She has white hair and beautiful blue eyes. She just lit up the room when she laughed. He was more sedate, has a Charles Boyer accent. A charming couple. You must remember them."

"And you must remember that I didn't stay after the wedding ceremony. Had classes and work that day."

"Oh." She hesitated before closing the suitcase, giving his words thought. "I guess you're right, at that. You weren't a deputy yet. Anyway, they're the ones who invited us."

"Well *why* did they invite us? To an island, of all places. Becoming the Swiss family Robertson for a week isn't exactly my fondest dream."

"Robinson. It's the Swiss Family Robinson."

"Of course. A Swede would know that for sure."

"I guess I don't get the connection. Anyway, you don't want to go?"

"I didn't say that. It just seems odd to me, inviting the editorial staff and their spouses for a week. It must be a big house. How many are going?"

Astrid counted on her fingers while she gave him the names.

"Besides Helena and Eddie are her nephew, of course, Marvin and Dee; Charlie and Jenny Hart; Will and Geena; and you and me. That's all. Makes ten altogether."

"Must be a *really* good-sized house."

"Dee said it has eight bedrooms and nine bathrooms, plus beds in an attic room for children when they visit. I guess the man who built it planned to open a small hotel or bed and breakfast, but then he became ill and never went through with it. Don't worry. They have plenty of room. Dee said the aunt inherited the place. It's worth a fortune now. She got that summer home and her brother, Marvin's father, got the newspaper and commercial printing businesses. Besides that, a bundle of money was divided between them. I expect we'll be put up in style, and have fun on the beach and just roaming the island. Do you play tennis, Abram?"

He shuddered.

"Tennis! Well, you see," he said in a dandified affectation, jutting his jaw, "Daddums thought I should take tennis lessons, but Mater insisted on ballet lessons. In the end, they couldn't agree, so I settled it by going out for street football with the local gang."

Her glaring look said more than spoken words.

"You could just say no."

"Okay. No, I don't play tennis."

"Well, at least we can swim and enjoy sunbathing, take walks. And don't forget that we'll have fresh lobster."

"I sure hope Larry doesn't have to call me back to Fairchance."

"And I hope you mean that."

Astrid shut the lid on her case and transferred it to the lounge chair where she could add items in the remaining days before leaving. She hoped Abram would be able to stay with her all week despite his apparent reluctance about the island vacation. She knew the underlying problem…he had no love for salt water. Now that he was a deputy sheriff, he worked odd hours, but Larry had said he deserved a vacation. Only a natural disaster, a murder, or the outbreak of war would cause him to order Abram back to work, he had said.

You'd better mean that, Astrid mumbled.

"What?"

"Nothing. I guess I'm ready to go."

"About time," Abram said.

She checked the black over-shoulder bag she always carried.

"Okay. Let's go."

In the kitchen, they stopped for a glass of water.

"I hope the weather will be good on the island," she said.

"I expect rain all week. After all, it's your vacation. Things just can't go right."

"Well I must say. Not everything bad follows me, Abram."

"Could'a fooled me."

He was about to lock the kitchen door behind them when the phone rang.

"Right on cue," he said. "You or me?"

He got to the phone first, listened a few seconds, and said, "We'll be right there."

"What is it?" she asked.

"A drowning at the college. A couple of kids were swimming and decided to race across the lake. One went down and didn't come up."

"Oh God. Fourth of July celebration and someone has to show off and get himself drowned."

"That's about it," he said.

"I'll drive," Astrid said before he could get into the driver's seat.

He seldom drove her Jeep but wouldn't think of riding without buckling up when she drove. They all but flew over the road to the hillside turn and downward.

"Don't forget there's a stop sign at the bottom," Abram said. Even he heard the desperation in his own voice.

"I know. I always stop there."

"That's reassuring."

More than once he jammed his foot hard against the floorboard as they sailed to the college road and on to a quick stop in the parking lot.

"Wait a minute while my clothes catch up," he said.

"You make it sound like I drive too fast."

"Well?"

"I'm not a fast driver. I was going just…"

The rest was muffled.

"How's that again?"

"Never mind. Was it Larry who called?"

"No. It was Deputy Brown."

"And just the one boy drowned?"

"Yeah. Just the one. He didn't know the name yet."

A crowd of all ages, children and adults, had gathered on the shore of the sparkly, clear lake. The college, a collection of brown wood classroom and dormitory buildings along a plateau on a gradual incline above the lake, was the site of the annual Fourth of July fair that always concluded with nighttime fireworks. Abram studied the colorful booths and the food pavilion, a gala scene now mostly void of customers due to the drowning. He had the fleeting memory of how he'd longed to get here and sample a few of those mouth-watering goodies. Instead, he lost his appetite listening to the murmurs: *So tragic...Where were their parents?...I'm taking my kids home... Did anyone call the police yet?*

"I see Larry and Beth over there by the pavilion, Abram," Astrid said. "I'll just quickly interview a few bystanders here if you want to go check in with him."

"Okay. Catch up with you later."

She hurried down to the lake to get some on-the-scene reactions. This would increase the tension at *The Bugle* on this very busy weekend. Ordinarily the three reporters could plan a bit of relaxation over weekends. *Just before a wonderful week at the island, this has to happen. What a bummer. Wonder if we will still go, although I can't see what particular good it would do for us to remain here.*

The first man and woman she approached tried to avoid eye contact with her. He held his wife by the arm and squinted against the bright sunlight over the lake, as if he could see the tragedy as it was happening. His white short-sleeve shirt had a smear of mustard on the front. His wife obviously didn't mind showing skin, though Astrid had seen far more shapely legs. They looked spindly under a body that could be treacherously close to toppling over under an amazing bust, about two cup sizes larger than her own. Might be that she was a carnival sideshow feature about 20 years ago, Astrid thought.

"Excuse me. I'm Astrid Lincoln, news editor at *The Bugle*. Do you know if these were local boys?"

"Local boys?" The man flashed an angry look at her. "Hell, no, I don't know if they were local boys. I just know someone should pay for this tragedy. The college should be sued. Why wasn't there a lifeguard on duty? Huh? Can you tell me that? Why wasn't there a boat alongside them? They had a damned nice fair going here, and because of neglect, it turned into tragedy of the worst kind. They shouldn't have allowed swimming today. None of these kids should have to witness this. I sent my two girls home with their aunt. Got them out of here. Just look around. Parents and kids watching like it was an outdoor movie. Disgusting."

"What's your name, sir?"Astrid asked.

"My name is Richard Monteith."

Astrid knew it would be best to hold her tongue, but couldn't resist.

"Why did you stay to watch and not go home with your daughters?"

Now the missus whirled about and took up his harangue. Astrid almost reached to steady her in what looked like a recklessly dangerous move.

"We have a right to be here. We want to see first-hand who the victim is. You reporters. What makes you so worthy and not us? Just because you report gossip for that rag newspaper? We'll stay as long as we want to."

Guess you didn't notice the tape recorder in my hand, Astrid thought. Smiling politely, she walked on. *Some people really deserve to be quoted in the newspaper.*

The day dragged on, while Astrid gathered quotes from shocked fair-goers and Abram assisted Sheriff Larry Knight and Deputy Brown as well as city police officers Marsh and Holmes and Police Chief Rawleigh with fact-finding and crowd control. By late evening, Astrid and Abram were back in their hillside home, their own paradise. They ate a late pick-up meal before sitting quietly in the den, staring at the blaze-less fireplace.

"What a terrible tragedy," Astrid said when she could no longer just silently re-live the day at the lake.

"Sure was. Never saw the campus so still before. What those parents must be going through. You know the worst of it? The college had put up a sign telling visitors that no swimming was allowed. But the kids knocked it print-side down, so they wouldn't be told swimming wasn't allowed."

"Kids. They're so reckless," Astrid said.

"They have no idea how quickly life can be lost."

Astrid often wondered if Abram would like to have children, but the topic was somehow off limits in their conversations. She thought maybe he would mention it sometime. For now, her mind went back to the angry crowd at the lake. They were all so quiet at first, then the murmurs became louder and louder, until it seemed that they might storm the college president's office. They might have, too, if he had been there, but someone said he was out of town.

"You'll work tomorrow, will you Abram?"

"Right," he said with a heavy sigh. "I don't know why. There's nothing more we can do. But Larry asked me to go in, so I said I would."

"He seems to rely on you a lot lately, doesn't he?"

"I guess he does. Pretty well staffed now, so I don't know why he should call on me so much."

"I do. It's because you've proved what a good deputy you are. He knows when he's got a good thing."

"Yeah. I guess I am a *thing* at that."

"Abram! You know what I mean."

He could be so aggravating at times.

CHAPTER 2

Astrid waited by the phone for Abram's call. This summer cottage, as Helena Reese referred to it, couldn't be more beautiful and impressive at first sight, set on carpet-smooth green lawn, sprinkled with colorful flower gardens, high over the water at the end of the island. Inside, the aroma of hardwood and flowers filled large rooms mainly furnished in white. All main floor rooms except the library had bay windows or wide picture windows for panoramic views of the bay, islands, a variety of birds, and colorful boats. The ten-acre property dropped sharply to a boathouse and dock below.

But in all this grandeur, only one telephone. She and Abram had agreed that she would wait for his call at night, since it wasn't certain when he'd be home from work. He should be here with her, but everything went crazy after the drowning at Fairchance College.

The boy's identity was soon passed along among spectators once someone said it was Mayor Nathan Demetrie's son Billy. His friend, Tab Enfield, was inconsolable, sobbing that his father would kill him for swimming in the lake and why did Billy egg him on to race? Abram and Larry contacted Tab's father, who arrived on the scene within 15 minutes. Contrary to what the boy feared, his dad took him in his arms and told him he wasn't in trouble. The two teenagers wore bathing trunks under their jeans when they went to the fair on their bikes without telling their parents. They had let a few friends know that they planned to race for the other shore, so several students saw the incident.

The scene became chaotic when the mayor arrived. Abram told Astrid he thought he might have to take the man into custody before he hurt someone in his out-of-control anguish. However, when Mrs. Demetrie arrived, still wearing curlers from the beauty shop, Mayor Demetrie had someone to share grief with. Ranting more would accomplish nothing. The couple watched while divers searched for the body.

Though *The Bugle*'s front page carried pictures from a few Fourth of July events around the county, the tragic drowning at the fair took precedence. Astrid worked into the night with Charlie and Will both Sunday and Monday. They were exhausted by Tuesday noon when the newspaper went to press, and they were ready for that much needed rest on the island. All except Will and his wife Geena rode with Marvin in his van. Astrid looked forward to this vacation with Abram, only to have him break the bad news that he wouldn't be going.

As if the drowning weren't enough tragedy for the weekend, Abram came home Monday night with still more bad news.

"This has been a rough day, Hon," he said as he collapsed into a recliner in the den.

"I'll bring supper on a tray. It's a cold one. Won't take any time to fix." Astrid said. "Just stay where you are and relax."

Because of the hot day, she had prepared a chicken and fruit salad, with iced tea. From the bakery, she had dinner rolls and, for dessert, cream puffs.

"You're almost asleep," she said on return.

"I'm okay. That looks real good. I'm hungry."

He ate most of his supper before he was ready to talk again. "Mmm. It *is* good."

Astrid noted his reluctance to tell her about his day, and soon learned why.

"There's been an abduction, Astrid. Two sisters were walking home from the country store out in Northam this afternoon when a car stopped and the driver called out the window for directions. The older sister went to the open back door to give them help. She was grabbed and pulled inside."

"Oh no, Abram. How awful."

"The younger sister, a 12-year-old, ran as soon as she saw what was happening. The car turned around and drove up behind her, but she had the good sense to run off the road into a wooded patch where the car couldn't go. She was close to home then and when she got there she found that her parents were gone. She called the farmers down the road about a mile, and found them there.

"They called the state police and, of course, they contacted us. We went out there. The girl could describe the car, but didn't get a good enough look at the driver, just that it was a woman. We haven't found them yet, but we'll resume search at daylight tomorrow. So you know what that means."

"No vacation time for you."

"No vacation for me or any of us. We'll be digging hard on this one."

Thinking about the whole scenario now, Astrid felt a deep-down dread. An abducted girl. Could they possibly find her?

"Of course, Abram. That poor girl. What she must be going through."

"Yeah."

His expression said more than his words; this was far too real for him. For just a few seconds he closed his eyes and laid back on the recliner.

"What is it, Abram? Something else, isn't it."

"Does it show? Oh…"

He covered his face with both hands and for a moment Astrid thought he would cry. She pulled a footstool to his side and reached for his hand.

"What? Tell me."

When he looked at her through eyes that saw a distant horror, he said, "I've never spoken of this to anyone, not even you. It's just too painful. I had a sister, a younger sister, who was the sweetest little girl you ever saw."

Astrid pulled back.

"A sister?"

"I should have told you, but like I said, it's almost more than I can bear to think of, even now. She looked to me as her protector--you know, big brother and all, despite the fact that we had an older brother. One day when we were fishing in the stream behind our house, she kept bugging me, calling out for me to see what she had found…that sort of thing. I told her to shut up and not scare the fish away. Several minutes went by and I didn't hear a sound from her. I thought she was just following my order. But after a while I became aware that she was nowhere in sight. I stood up and called her name, but she didn't answer. I started looking around the woods close by and calling her name. Still no answer. We were close to the road and I went out to it and called and called. Then I panicked and ran back to the house. No one had seen her. Needless to say, I cried and cried. My parents thought I might have to be sedated. It was just too much knowing that I had not taken care of my little sister and that she had disappeared."

Astrid hated to see him in distress. She guessed what he would tell her.

"What happened to her?"

"I don't know. We never found out. Officers came and searched. Teams of men and women combed the woods where she disappeared. Everyone in town was watching for her. When it became obvious that they weren't going to find her and that she hadn't drowned, each day became more unbearable. For a year, I kept going back to the area where I last saw her and continued to hunt for her. She had just literally disappeared. Maybe she decided to walk home by herself and someone grabbed her. To this day, I can't believe she's dead. But if not, what happened to her? If she died, how? Did she suffer? Those questions never go away. They haunt me still."

"How old was she?"

"Seven. I was 12. She would be 27 now. All those years…"

"I understand, Abram."

As she thought about that conversation now, Astrid felt the same horror, the same sense of helplessness that Abram had. She stood up to walk off her anguish. It was a luxurious library with three walls of books predominating. Two green leather chairs and floor lamps on each side of the narrow window, a rolling stepladder to reach top shelves, well padded dark green rug…what every summer cottage should have. And that wonderful scent of leather pervading the entire room. It was delicious.

She never was overwhelmed by opulence since Grandfather Thorpe insisted on a clean, neat home, but no frills, not even lace curtains at the windows. She became acquainted with the poor farmers' children at school and visited and played with them in their unbelievably shabby homes, but never felt above them, even though her family was wealthy. She understood the value of life above all else. To think of a child's being mistreated raised her ire like nothing else. In that, she and Abram were the same. He would be devastated if he found the dead body of the missing girl. But what about the alternative? What if she were found and admitted to having been sexually abused? She would be haunted for the rest of her life. And it would conjure up more terrible fears about his little sister's fate. Astrid rolled her head trying to dismiss the picture she had of the horror of being young and in the hands of evil men and women.

"He hasn't called yet?"

Astrid jumped at the sound of Dee's voice.

"I didn't hear you come in," Astrid said, sitting down on one of the two green chairs. "Thought you had gone to bed."

Dee went to the other chair.

"It really is too early for me, even though I'm sleepy. Marvin is fast asleep. I thought I'd see if you were still up."

"I'm surprised you could find me."

"Ha! I know what you mean. This is quite the *little* summer house, all right. Marvin said he used to come here as a boy and always loved it. We had a funny discussion about getting here back then. I asked him if he had to row a boat across from the mainland, and he said no, they just swam across with rope in their teeth to pull a dinghy behind. He added that they had to fight the Indians once they got across, of course."

Astrid laughed. She had told Dee about the abducted girl, and understood that she was trying to keep her from thinking about it.

"Helena will probably show us around," Astrid said. "I don't know about your room, but mine is huge. We could hold a dance in there. I don't mean to be catty, but you'd think they could install a few more telephones around the house."

"Maybe an island home like this was meant to be isolated. Likely they don't want to hear from anyone. An island retreat would certainly keep most friends and neighbors away."

"I should have brought my new mobile phone. It just didn't seem like I'd need it other than for this one call each day."

"I don't have one of those yet," Dee said. "Seems a bit unhandy to me, so big and bulky."

"Just a bit. I don't know what's keeping Abram so late. It's 10:30 already. He never got home this late from work. But, of course, he's never been on this kind of case before, either."

"It's too bad this had to happen right now—or ever, for that matter. I know you never really had your honeymoon. This would have been such a great time for you two."

Astrid had never given thought to their lost honeymoon, not since returning early from Florida to Maine because it was so cold and miserable there. They were happy in their own home in Fairchance.

"That's what I thought," she lied. "But now that he's a deputy sheriff, he has to do his duty. That's who he is, you know, always conscientious."

"I know. Just like you."

Astrid knew before he went into law enforcement that Abram would be a good deputy. His instincts were almost always correct, unlike her own, and he had an analytical mind, able to sort out important facts from trivia.

"Not so sure about myself," she said. "Anyway, you and Marvin will have a second honeymoon. It was so nice of his Aunt Helena to do this. You never did say where you went on your real honeymoon last year, Dee."

She saw the blush, as Dee considered whether to tell her now. Astrid could say that she looked up to Dee. However, the considerable difference in their heights meant that physically Dee had to do the looking up. Short and gorgeous was how Astrid described her friend. She must have been a ball of fire when she was younger, because she still had more energy than most 20-year-olds. To think of her owning and operating an alcoholics rehabilitation camp for 10 years was mind boggling. Ten years of that difficult work had put some gray in her black hair, but it hadn't lessened her spirit.

"We didn't go very far," Dee finally replied, "just to my country home in Twin Ports. Neither of us thought it was necessary to travel a long way when we both had a private house where we could be together in peace and quiet. We've both traveled enough not to feel the need to go to an exotic honeymoon villa, or whatever. Honeymooners never see the sights, anyway."

"You're so right," Astrid said, still thinking how unpleasant her honeymoon was. "You didn't want to go to Marvin's mountain top home?"

"He doesn't like to go there since that terrible accident. That's why I suggested mine."

The accident that took his first wife's life. Naturally it would have put a damper on the honeymoon to be in the place that his late, paraplegic wife loved so much. Astrid hadn't meant to be insensitive to that fact, yet there it was. Just slipped out. Dee understood as usual, and for that Astrid was thankful.

"I thought Will and Geena would be here by now," Dee said.

"He thought so, too, but at the last minute he received a telephone call. He was very mysterious about it, and I do know it had nothing to do with sports. I don't want to say anything that may be totally wrong, Dee, but I suspect he's scouting for a new job."

"Oh dear. He's such a good reporter and writer. He'll be hard to replace."

"Please don't repeat this because I'm only guessing. He talked for a while, then said he'd call right back, and ran up the stairs to your office for privacy. Anyway, when he came back he told me that something had come up. He said he'd try to get over here before the end of the week. I'm glad you spoke of it. I'm so wrapped up in my own thoughts I just about forgot to tell you."

Dee was about to say more when the phone rang. She patted Astrid's arm.

"That will be Abram. I'll go now. Talk with you another time."

"See you at breakfast," Astrid said as she reached for the phone.

CHAPTER 3

How she hoped he would tell her the search was over, and that all was well. More than coming here, that would be an enormous relief for all concerned.

"Abram? Any news ?"

"No. We've been interviewing all the friends of the family, townspeople who knew them, anyone at all who might know something. But nothing has opened up."

"I'm so sorry. You couldn't even find the car? You said the sister had a good description of it."

"She knew it was a big one, old, green. But didn't know the make. We think it may be an Olds. No one we could find has seen one around there. It's one of those things, you know. Could be that several have seen it, but few really take note of a random vehicle driving around."

"Unless there's something unusual about it."

"True. The only thing she could say was that a man and a woman were inside and that the woman had long stringy hair, possibly dark blond. She saw the man in the back seat reach out for her sister and pull her inside. And then, of course, she ran for her own safety."

"Did you tell me their names?"

"I don't think so. Parents are Delwin and Bertha Neal. The older daughter is Miriam and the younger one is Angela. Poor Angela. She's so upset that she's sick today. I know how she feels."

They were silent for a long few minutes before Abram said, "There's got to be a way to flush them out. The Neals don't have money, so they can't expect to get a ransom for Miriam. That leaves only one of three things."

"To sell her in the flesh trade," Astrid chimed in, "keep her as a slave for themselves, or…"

When she hesitated, Abram finished, "Abuse, then murder."

"It's terrifying to think of, Abram."

"The worst of it is that every day, every hour we can't find them, the less likely we ever will."

"Has Larry put on more deputies?"

"Not yet. But he's driving us as hard as he can. I just got out of the last briefing, and he wants us back at eight tomorrow morning. They have a couple of good, experienced bloodhounds they'll use. I can't see that they'll help any. They were in a car, for God sake."

Profanity was so out of character for Abram, but she understood. Frustration at a peak, probably everyone at the sheriff's office was ready to lash out.

Another long pause, then Abram spoke more cheerfully.

"Nice there, is it? All that you expected?"

"You should see it. Unbelievable. I hope you'll be able to get here."

"I hope so, too. I need to eat something now and try to get some sleep. By-the-way, who's minding your shop this week? Dee didn't shut down the newspaper office, did she?"

"Didn't I tell you? I'm surprised Larry didn't say. Beth took over, and Dee has given her the go-ahead to bring in someone she knows with newspaper experience. I'll bet Larry didn't even notice that she wasn't home."

She repeated, "I do hope you can come over, even for a day."

"I'll be there if I can. It's been a long day, Sweetheart. I need to get some shut-eye. Above all, you get plenty of rest and have a good time."

"Not much danger of doing anything different." Astrid said. "It's very, very quiet here except for the sounds of sea water washing in and out, crashing over rocks below. You hear that swoosh, swoosh with windows open. I think this could become addictive."

After they said goodbye, Astrid sat staring at the phone, wishing she could somehow help find that poor girl. No one should just vanish like that. No one should become a non-person, and Miriam would be just that, if she lived.

She had painted this island home to Abram as addictive, but she lied. There was only so much swoosh, swoosh anyone could take without turning into a babbling dingbat. She realized now that her real addiction was to snoop around in a prime case. But here on the island she felt cut off from the real world. Nothing happened here. She could step outside and yell and no one would hear her. If she tried to relax and feel at peace, she would never get beyond the fact that Abram faced daily pressure doing his best to search for the missing teenager.

Getting to her feet, she wandered from the library to the kitchen, poured herself a drink of water, rinsed the glass and set it upside down on the spotless light wood drain board. A door to a wide open-air porch looked inviting. Fresh air might lift her spirits.

Damp, salty gusts of air whistled around corners. She hugged herself for warmth. Breezes blew almost constantly on this high, jutting point of the island, and while there were no black flies, it felt cold. She remembered that the farm had plenty of those stingy little monsters. Somewhere out in the long reach of bay, a bell buoy clanged to warn sailors of dangerous rocks.

Though she couldn't see the shore below from this porch, she could hear the crash of waves echo off the boulders. Swoosh in, bang, swoosh out. Over and over again. Sounds here differed from anything she knew when she lived on the farm. There, she would sit on the porch late at night like this and hear fox pups yelp and whine in the woods, cows shuffle and snort in the barn, a whippoorwill repeat its own name from a safe perch just out of human sight. The fragrance of clover and fresh-mown hay under a bright, cloudless sky could touch her emotions to the point of tears.

Helena had described the island air as refreshing. Astrid felt its bracing effect at times. But at low tide, wafts of fishy air and sometimes a suggestion of sewer weren't exactly stimulating. She preferred a hot country night with sweet lilac perfume to this cold, sharp, odiferous atmosphere.

A poet might describe this moonlit night as a time to reflect. Would the howling wind be painted as the sound of drowned fishermen's voices objecting to their watery graves? Would a poet see phantom ships on the black water, their captains trying to avoid rock formations under the siren promise of calm passage and sure safety to their island homes? A more poetic soul might imagine ghosts belching wisps of icy air on her face. And don't forget the specks of light along the mainland shores. Maybe they twinkle for the sole purpose of guiding sailors home through dead doldrums or raging storm. Moonlit paths over the water could be lanterns along the inky road of bottomless despair, lighting routes to happy days.

Shaking off the mesmerizing introspection, she thought, *Where did that nonsense come from?* She shivered and wondered what this place did to her. Maybe it was peaceful horror.

What a crazy oxymoron. What kind of idiot am I, standing in this frigid air and letting my mind wander? Time to go to bed. Now!

As she reached for the doorknob, she hesitated when she heard the hollow call of a loon from what could be an inland lake. She could swear she heard the name Miriam in that mournful wail. Her skin crawled with a million goosebumps and she hurried inside to shut out all the weird thoughts that had invaded her mind on a lonely island night by the sea.

*****

Beth felt at home sitting in the editor's chair. From the first day she worked in *The Bugle* office after arriving in Fairchance, she knew journalism suited her. Except, of course, that episode on the golf course when she had to photograph a woman's body with slashed throat. That first assignment did give her a bit of concern about her future here. However, not long after that she began to feel the excitement of being the first to know, so to speak, and to impart the news to the public. That intoxicating rush kept her working here until after marrying Larry Knight. Then the baby became her one and only interest. But here she was again, pretending to be editor for a few days.

While she read Charlie's list of stories for her to follow up during his five-day absence, she once again lapsed into memory of the poignant moment when she told Larry she would marry him. It was no quick decision, and she did have qualms about leaving work that she liked so well. Sometimes, even now, the urge flooded back to return to full-time journalism, to interview people, just to interact with more people.

As much as she liked the work, however, she wouldn't give up her life with Larry and little Howie. If ever she made a right move, accepting his proposal was it. Still, here she was substituting for the editor, and happy for the respite from that wonderful, sometimes frustrating, son of theirs.

Right now, she had to focus on the dreadful kidnap case Larry was working on. She did wish that Astrid were here. She was so much better at that sort of story.

"You're far-away."

She snapped out of her reverie when her old friend spoke.

"Griff. So nice of you to come."

She stood up, with her hand out in greeting. She had heard from a mutual friend that Griff and his wife Faith were to be at a summer camp in the area. She called him on the off-chance that he might come in and help. They had worked together for a college campus newspaper several years ago.

"I'm afraid I was daydreaming, Griff."

"I can see that married life agrees with you. You're more beautiful than you were in college."

She wanted to return the compliment, but couldn't honestly say he looked great. It had been years since they'd seen each other, so it was a bit of a shock to see how he had aged, perhaps looking older because of the graying ring of hair surrounding a shiny bald head, to say nothing of a pronounced slouch. But his gray-brown eyes were as playful as they were in college.

"Always the flatterer. College! How many years ago was that? It's so good of you to come and help me out this week."

"Hey, any time. At least, any time I'm in the state of Maine. Fishing will always be there, and Faith has enough to keep her busy with all the activities the camp has planned each day. Besides, we'll have one more week after this one."

"I never heard of a camp for adults like that so I didn't know we had one nearby. Aren't your children heartbroken not to get to Maine for swimming and fishing?'

"Nah. The two boys have baseball and swimming at the Y, and Abigail is the little princess who will be pampered and petted by her grandmother. One thing about the Hartford area, there's a lot for kids to do. They probably will be happy to have Mom and Dad out of the house so they can stay up late and eat all the junk food they want."

Beth laughed. Her Howie was always happy to go with his aunt, but he looked for his mom when it came to being tucked in at night, or needing sympathy over a scraped knee.

"I just can't believe that you two have three children," she said.

"Me neither." He looked around. "Now, where do you want me to work?"

"Take the desk facing mine." She pointed to Astrid's desk. "We'll play editor and associate for the week. It won't be nearly as exciting as your police beat in the city, but you will really be helping an old friend out."

He adjusted the chair and settled in to work. Griff had an ever- present serious scowl, an expression he had even in college when the two of them dated for a brief period. Along with the scowl, deep lines furrowed his face, the same face she had thought so perfect at one time.

"Did you read last week's newspaper?" she asked. "Read about the drowning?"

"I did. And I didn't see anything too earthshaking that I can't handle."

"Well, be prepared to be shaken. Since then, we have an abduction in a nearby village. A 14-year-old girl was snatched as she and her sister walked along the country road. You don't know my husband Larry. He's the sheriff. Most of his deputies and police in the city are searching for any sign of the girl. State police are also on alert, of course.

"No sign of her yet? How long has she been missing?"

"Since yesterday. I know the odds of her survival the longer she's missing. She and her 12-year-old sister had been shopping at the general store, and were walking home together. Seems that the younger one didn't go near the car when it stopped ostensibly to ask for directions. When she saw them snatch her sister, she ran and managed to get home to tell her parents."

"Can she tell the cops much?"

"No, I'm afraid not. Of course, we'll cover it, but I'm afraid the dailies are all over it as usual. Larry said they had to call all the media in order to get the word out to call authorities if anyone has seen anything."

"Of course."

"You know all about this sort of thing. Do you get many cases like it in the city? How long have you been a police officer, anyway?"

"I've been on this job for six years. We haven't had many kidnappings, only a couple for ransom. And we had one teenager who was never found. Have the parents received a ransom demand?"

"No. But that could change any time, I suppose. I think the first thing you should do is see Larry before he gets away from the office. It's 8:30. He should still be there. Someone has to cover the office, so I'll work here. There isn't much else going on. I can take care of all that. Take the camera at the other desk. I presume you take photos?"

"Oh yes. It's required police procedure. Is there anything else I should know before I go?"

"Yeah. You should know how to get around Fairchance."

Beth reached in a desk drawer for a city map.

"It's not difficult. Streets are well laid out." She spread it out and showed him where Larry's office was. "You can take the map. It will be handy."

He left, obviously fired up over the case. Perhaps he'd thought he would be asked to write town briefs or some such thing. She recalled that he was a good reporter, wrote accurately and well, and was good at meeting deadlines.

An hour later, she was about to read Charlie's editorial that he had written yesterday before going to the island. She let the phone ring twice before reaching for it.

The familiar voice said, "Hi Beth."

Beth smiled.

"Hi Astrid."

Astrid said. "How's it going? Are you okay?"

"I'm fine. Griff has already gone out to gather what he can on the kidnap case."

"Did you tell me he's a policeman in Hartford?"

"That's right. But we worked together on a newspaper, and he went into a newspaper office after graduation even while he was studying Criminal Justice."

"He'll know just what to do then."

"He will. So, how is it going with you, Astrid? Are you enjoying your retreat?"

From the silence, Beth had to believe it wasn't just what Astrid expected.

"Astrid?"

"Oh, ya. It's nice here. The house is magnificent. I've never seen a cottage this large and well furnished. But I do miss Abram, I guess. It seems just too quiet."

"This is only your first full day, and it's early. Do they have a nice beach?"

"No. They tell me it's not a really nice one. Just a small patch of sand that they cleared of rocks so they could swim. I haven't tried it yet. I don't know. The salt water was never a great attraction for me. It's too cold. I did think I'd like boating on it, but Dee hasn't said anything about doing that yet. Maybe we'll get out on a lobster boat."

Beth looked toward the door when a church club woman she recognized entered and walked over to her desk, said nothing when she saw that a phone conversation was going on, simply deposited an announcement, and left.

"Someone just come in? You need to hang up?" Astrid asked.

"No. Kathryn DeJohn just left a club meeting notice. So have you gone for a walk yet to look around the island?"

"Not yet. I'll go soon. There's a small store a couple of miles up the road. I'll go over there and get a few snacks for the evening. There isn't much food here."

She snorted.

"I thought we'd have everything, but it appears that they haven't stocked up very well. Supper last night was from a can. Beans, at that. Beans and brown bread."

Beth moaned.

"Maybe they want you to catch your own supper in the bay."

Astrid roared.

"I think you're right. However, I guess not. If I can find a lobsterman with lobsters for sale, I'll buy some for all of us. Oh, here comes Charlie. I'll bet he wants to talk with you."

The next voice was Charlie's.

"Has anyone interviewed the family yet?"

"And good morning to you, Charlie."

"Huh? Oh, yeah. Good morning, Beth."

"Griff will go out there with Larry and Abram."

They hadn't talked extensively about what he would do, but she had every confidence in his reporting instinct. No need to tell Charlie any different.

"I was thinking," Charlie said. "Someone should back up from the time of the kidnapping on the road. Check out where the girls were before that and find those who saw them. Someone might have seen that car hanging around the area. Maybe they'd have noticed if the driver was watching the girl."

"Good thinking, Charlie. I'll see to it that Griff does that. Possibly they've already checked, but he can ask."

In fact, she knew they had checked it out, but no need to act smart-assed over it.

"We should be there to do our part, but it wouldn't be right to leave. Dee and Marvin would be insulted, and I, for one, would be in the dog house. Jenny has wanted me to take off a week like this for a long time."

"Of course. We'll be okay, and we'll do our best to dig out all we can. Relax. Astrid says it's nice and quiet there. You can all enjoy that. Don't even think about the office. If there are any developments, I'll call you."

She heard Astrid in the background.

"Astrid wants to say something. I'll leave you two now."

Beth pulled the phone away from her ear when Astrid came on the line. She thought possibly Astrid could be heard from there without a phone. She had actually toned down her volume since the first time Beth met her, but she still put out more decibels than the average person.

"No one is with you, Beth?"

"No. I'm alone."

"Charlie left the room. I wanted to say this to you quietly, just the two of us."

Beth smiled. Astrid saying something quietly?

"Last night, after I talked with Abram, I started to go to my room when I passed a small porthole window in the hallway upstairs. I saw it when we arrived and thought what a clever touch. So I stopped and took a look out. In the darkness, I saw a light that I supposed came from a lighthouse. Then I thought it could be a light from a boat. Well, this morning I looked again, and there was no lighthouse and no boats over that way, only a hillside across the inlet. I could see nothing. It's bugging me, because there's no apparent way a light could have come from there."

"Really! So I expect you're going to investigate further."

"Well, of course. It's too weird to let it go by."

"Oh, Astrid. If there isn't a problem, you go looking for one. Well, good luck and stay out of trouble. Please."

"You don't have to worry about me."

I'm afraid I do, given your track record.

After they said their goodbyes, Beth checked out the Main Street view from her desk. Creating a newspaper office out of a Cape house was clever, but the best part of it was this wonderful overview of Main Street the editorial room provided. With school out, students took advantage of their free time to shop at what used to be the Five and Dime store, now offering a higher grade of clothing. A handful of youngsters studied the various kittens and puppies being displayed in a just-opened pet store. She grinned when a mother grabbed her son's arm and dragged him away, scolding all the time. No doubt he'd begged for a puppy. Beth had a similarly hard time convincing Howie that when he was older he could have a puppy. He wanted one now, of course.

She heard the outside back door slam and heavy footsteps coming down the hallway. Time to get back to work. As she turned back to her computer, she had a fleeting thought about Astrid's searching for the cause of a mysterious light on Twilight Isle. Of course it was nothing to worry about, just Astrid's search for some trivial adventure when everything was quiet and dull. Still...

CHAPTER 4

B y lunchtime Helena and Eddie had returned from shopping in town, and laid out what Astrid called real food for lunch: hamburgers that Marvin grilled in the kitchen, bakery buns, and salads. It was agreed to eat lunch on the sun porch with its unobstructed view of the bay, smaller islands, and the mainland hillsides. Like being perched in a lookout tower, the room had nothing around it—no trees, no buildings, no hills.

Astrid was reluctant to distance herself from the others, but since everyone was coupled up, she took one of several TV stands and found an empty space on the right side of the window seat. Out here on the porch, it was impossible to see the hillside where she had noticed the light last night. Her room and that bit of hallway were on the west side over the garages, remote from the other rooms. This morning she wandered around that end of the house and discovered another stairway, not a secret one, but likely for servants to be able to leave the house without being seen or heard elsewhere. Likely it was used years ago. Now there were few servants, probably only those who came in from island homes during daytimes. The full time caretaker and his wife resided in the modest cottage beyond the last of the four garages. They hadn't made an appearance yet, Helena said, because they were both recuperating from flu. That accounted for the scarcity of food in the house.

"Eating alone?" Dee said. "I'll have lunch with you, Astrid."

"Good. I could use company. Marvin and Eddie are hitting it off well, I see."

"Marvin told me he never did get very well acquainted with Eddie. I guess his Aunt Helena usually visited the family when Marv was young and Eddie took care of the estate on Long Island. They're an interesting couple."

"Mmm."

"Helena's home base was with her parents on Long Island. Eddie enjoyed the grounds maintenance work there, Marvin told me, but did go with her any time she went overseas."

"Mmm."

"You're distracted, Astrid. Worried about Abram?"

"Not worried, I guess, so much as afraid he won't be able to come here at all. It would be nice for him to see this place. It's unique."

"Helena likes you. Maybe she'll invite the two of you over to the island later. She's a very generous woman."

"Maybe so." Astrid said.

She stood up to go to the buffet for lemonade. "You want something else? I'm getting lemonade."

"Yes, I'd like that, too, thanks."

She returned with the drinks, and they ate in silence until Dee asked, "Did you ever live near the water, Astrid?"

"No. As you know, I lived on a farm as a child and young adult, before going off to college."

"I love the sea. Twin Ports is a lovely small city, something like Fairchance. That's what I missed most during the ten years that I had the rehab camp, even though it was on a lake. To me, nothing compares to the salt water. Maybe when you're very young and live around it you never get over that special excitement just the smell of salt sea air gives you. I hope that Marvin and I will have a home on the bay, maybe when we retire."

Astrid looked up when Helena approached.

"You two can join the party, you know," she said.

"We're not hiding," Dee said. "Astrid came over here, and I decided to join her."

"Do you need anything?"

"No thanks." Astrid said. "But I do have a question."

"Yes? What's that?"

"Last night when I finished my phone call, close to 11 o'clock, I was on my way back to my room and looked out that porthole window. I saw a light glowing in the distance, apparently on the island. It looked to be coming from a house or cottage, but I couldn't really tell for sure. Since I didn't see any houses along the way as we came in, I was wondering what that's all about. It's not a lighthouse. I looked again this morning and couldn't see anything at all in that direction."

Helena appeared perplexed.

"I don't know. I never go to that side of the house any more. I can ask the caretaker when I see him. I expect it's a fisherman's tackle shack or boat house."

Dee snickered.

"Astrid is our eternal investigator," she explained. "Some might say snoop. She would like to have a mystery to solve everywhere she goes."

"Dee! How can you say that? I'm not...well, not always, anyway...a snoop."

She thought for a second, while Dee gave her the arched-eyebrow stare.

"Well, I guess I do have a healthier than normal curiosity."

"Healthier than normal? Who sneaks around a junk yard in the middle of the night and ends up being shot at?"

"That's interesting," Helena said. "You'll have to tell me about your investigations."

Dee stood up, and motioned for Helena to take her place.

"Since I know her adventures, I'll go back to Marvin and find out what he wants to do this afternoon."

"Don't forget that Eddie and I have planned a visit to a lobster shack at the other end of the island. I thought we could leave here at two."

"I'll keep that in mind," Dee said. "We can take a walk around the shore."

Astrid was disappointed. She wanted to get lobsters but had hoped to walk around to that place where the light shone, if she could find it. She'd have to leave it for another day. If Abram should come over to the island soon, she wouldn't get the chance to snoop, and that wouldn't do. For now, she would have to settle for visiting a real lobster shack, and bringing home fresh lobsters.

"I didn't know about the lobsters. I'd like to pay for them," she said. "We're cooking them here?"

"No, no. We'll get down and dirty and eat them hot, right out of the pot there. It's an outdoor operation with big pots for boiling the lobsters and eating at picnic tables. We haven't been there this year. Eddie and I enjoy it."

"That sounds super," Astrid said.

It wasn't exactly what she had in mind, but it *could* be fun, she decided.

"This is a beautiful spot," she said. "Just look at the bay. So calm it looks like a giant mirror with the hillside trees and blue sky reflections."

Helena's smile showed a dreamy pride, Astrid thought, not so much in the wealthy nature of the place, but more of the environment, just as Astrid observed.

"You would have enjoyed the fireworks on the fourth," Helena said. "Across the bay they shot off colorful designs. I never saw anything like it. It was a calm night, a lot like right now. When a rocket would explode, all the trails of color came alive in the sky and on the water. But it's not always calm like this," Helena said. For a moment, she fell into deep thought, as if seeing a memorable, but unpleasant, incident. "Sometimes, it can get nasty--squally, dark, wild. Very dangerous."

Her voice had turned eerily mellow. She shook herself loose from the reflection, and her smile returned in all its vibrance.

"Let's hope you don't experience that wildness during your vacation this week. Now, tell me what sorts of things you do that cause Dee to say you're a snoop."

Astrid liked Helena. Considering her worldly travels, she might also be snoopy, though she couldn't possibly be as likely to get into similar troubles. More likely she found success wherever she went. That conclusion was based on no particular reason other than that she commanded attention by just walking into a room. Astrid saw herself neither more nor less than anyone else. But in Helena, she recognized a greatness that very few people had. It wouldn't be difficult to imagine her as the president of the United States, a world leader to be reckoned with.

"My friends tease me because a couple of the stories I've gone after have taken me into difficult situations," Astrid said. "I've been shot at, yes. And I suffered a few knife wounds, I got caught in a bear trap that gave me some injury but not serious. My house was blown up by a crazy neighbor who thought a lot of money had been hidden in the cellar. Sometimes I've gotten into a mess because I tried to help a good friend."

Astrid thought particularly about Holly and her comeback from the devastating deaths of her parents. She and her newly found biological dad had come a long way. Astrid recently heard that Holly would soon be married.

"There are times, though, that things turn out really well." She shrugged. "It all balances out, I'd say."

Helena tipped her head back and laughed.

"I know what you mean," she said. "It's so true. Eddie and I are living examples of that."

What did that mean? Astrid wanted to ask, but decided for once not to be too inquisitive. If Helena wanted to reveal some problem she and her husband had faced, then she would. For now, it was good just to hear her talk and laugh and be as down-to-earth as everyone else. Somehow, though, Astrid had the feeling that behind her comfortable presence lay a complex individual with more stories to tell than Astrid would ever have.

"If you're really interested in that light you saw," Helena said, "I'll take you over that way tomorrow morning. You have my curiosity roused, too. What do you say? Shall we become a pair of Nancy Drews for a day?"

"Oh, I like that. Ya, it would be fun."

"Remember the Nancy Drew TV series?"

"No, I'm afraid not. I read her books, though."

"Funny how in one generation everything changes so. Doesn't take long before those programs we used to enjoy are no longer popular. They seem old-fashioned and ridiculous. Likely in several years to come people will say today's shows are stupid. I saw that new show *Northern Exposure* a couple weeks ago and thought it was funny. What will it look like in another 20 years, I wonder."

"Did you see *Keeping Up Appearances* on PBS? I think that will always be funny. Human nature doesn't change that much—just look at history."

Helena laughed and everyone on the porch turned to see what was so funny. Eddie started toward them.

"You two seem to be in high spirits over here. Is it a private party?"

Astrid loved that French accent. She sensed it wasn't strictly French, but her knowledge of foreign dialects was limited.

"Come, sit with us," Helena said. "We're just commenting on cultural changes and TV programs years ago. What will future generations think of programs we watch today?"

"Can you find anything but unrealistic shows today?" he asked.

"Not likely. Dee claims that Astrid is the investigative type. The word she used was snoop."

"Snoop is she?" Eddie wrapped his hand around Helena's and in a lowered voice said, "Then maybe we're in trouble, my dear?"

The sly look that passed between them couldn't be mistaken. They shared a secret. Sometimes it was just so difficult for Astrid to remain mute when her curiosity was aroused. She had previously noticed their motions and quiet exchanges that could pass for coded understanding. Perhaps it was their closeness, intense eye contact, and whispers like young lovers that added up to odd behavior for a couple of their age, in Astrid's book. How she'd like to find out what rare bond they shared. As close as she and Abram were, their intimacy could never be interpreted as deep, dark, and secretive.

CHAPTER 5

Two o'clock arrived sooner than Astrid anticipated. She heard the old school bell, summoning guests to gather for the island tour and dinner at the lobster shack. Dee said she never liked lobster, so she was ambivalent about getting the critters, but she would enjoy the island sights. To Astrid, having lobster was a highlight of the island vacation, better than a T-bone steak.

In her oldest pair of blue jeans with a knee patch and a faded green polo shirt that Abram had discarded, she felt as comfortable as if she were going to the barn at the farm. While she put wallet in one pocket and a tissue in the other, her thoughts wandered to her brother and his transformation from a man with little interest in much of anything to one of superior management skill in operating the farm. At first, after Granddad died, Gunnar was anxious to sell the farm products business that he inherited, but the Axelgren Farms name had become popular in most grocery stores. Today Gunnar had nearly doubled the farm's production and markets. Once Astrid helped him with record keeping and work organization, he realized that it would be a gold mine for him and continued to build it up. She was proud of him.

She left the room and took the back stairway to the garage area where she found Helena and Eddie waiting beside what looked like a black hearse with rows of seats.

"What's this?" Astrid said. She walked over to take a closer look. "I heard it all the way upstairs. Whew. It's diesel."

"This is the island's taxi," Eddie said.

"It looks like a…"

"A hearse. Exactly," Helena said. "That's what it is, a converted hearse. What better taxi could you have? It gives a nice ride, and seats 10 or 12 people, good for visitors off the ferry with no one to pick them up."

"Is that a casket in back?"

"The driver has quite a sense of humor. Yes, he fashioned a luggage box to look like a casket. He needed something large to place supplies in. Islanders often have him pick up things for them on the mainland."

"Gives one a sense of security, for sure," Astrid said.

"The driver will point out landmarks along the way. We thought it would be better than as if we tried to do it. We'd miss points, I'm sure. And it gives us the freedom of being observers ourselves for a change."

While she talked, Dee and Marvin joined the party.

"Well look at this. Isn't this fun?" Dee said. "We get to take a ride in a hearse and have it as good as the deceased do."

"My dear!" Marvin said, "A bit disrespectful, aren't we?"

Astrid observed the twinkle in his eye and recalled when his first wife was killed in the auto he was driving on an icy road. The car careened off the mountainside road and he could do nothing to save her. He became withdrawn and thin, showed very little interest in the newspaper or the commercial printing business. Now he was a different man. He obviously adored Dee. He popped into the office daily, sometimes two or three times a day. He wasn't there about the newspaper, since he had sold it to Dee, but he bounded up the stairs to her office as if his business were urgent. Astrid turned her smile away from them, but she felt happy just thinking about what love does to people.

Charlie and Jenny came running. Astrid hadn't talked much with Jenny, but liked her. She was a bright, happy woman who appeared quite young. Dee had told her that she and Jenny were classmates and were the same age. Hard to believe.

"Sorry we're late," Charlie said. "I took what was supposed to be a brief nap. Jenny had to shake me awake."

"He's exhausted. This sea air got to him," Jenny said.

Charlie yawned. "Never been quite this tired. It must be the let-down. Can't remember when we had a vacation last."

"Well there," Helena said. "This vacation for all of you *was* a good idea."

"Surprising that I didn't wake up. The racket from the hearse is enough to wake the dead," he quipped.

Everyone groaned in unison. That was Charlie, an astute newspaper editor but the eternal wisecracker. To top it off, his downeast vernacular gave his quips an added sprinkling of humor.

The driver looked the part for driving a hearse. A little man with long white hair so thin his pink scalp showed through, he had thin lips and narrow eyes. He wore a black suit, white shirt, and black tie.

"If everyone's here," he said, "we can move on now. Welcome to Barrett's Bus Service. The biggest little taxi on the island."

"The only taxi on the island," Helena said with a laugh.

He sat behind the wheel and drove along the winding driveway to the main road before he picked up his microphone and announced, "I am Jeremy Barrett. Been on the island all my life. The island has about 500 real residents."

Astrid wondered who the unreal residents were and how many there were roaming the island. What did they look like?

"It's 200 square miles overall and 20 miles long. Locals follow routine habits, and I know them all. I can tell you where the Chapmans hide their money because they're still afraid banks will fail again."

If he hadn't announced that he'd lived a long time on the island, she would have guessed anyway from his strong downeast twang and speech pattern, minus r's, for one thing. If she had to decide which was more pure Maine dialect, Charlie or Barrett, she'd have to say the bus driver.

"I can name those who came back to the island," he continued, "after not doin' so great away. I guess they think it's a good place to hide. I know which lobstermen tempt fate by taking lobsters too small or too big from their traps. Depending on the Sunday of the month, I can recite the minister's sermon. He hasn't changed messages for 20 years. Gives the congregation time to catch a few winks. Some read and some knit. The minister don't care. The first Sunday of the month he brings out his love-thy-neighbor talk. The last Sunday, his stock sermon warns about the evils of drink and lust. Now that brings men awake long enough to snicker and wink at each other. These guys may look like dubbers but they know which way the wind blows."

Charlie called out, "Just your typical Maine town, then."

Laughter filled the bus. Astrid recalled that Abram and she had planned to go to church Sunday. Maybe they could make it yet if they could just locate Miriam. How Angela must be hurting with the memory of seeing her sister snatched off the roadway when she could do nothing but run for help.

"That's about it. Marriages, divorces, abusive husbands...I can tell it all. Over there, beyond the tall hedge, is Bella Beaumont's cottage. She's a do-gooda, always wanting to give someone a bit of her baking. If she offers any to you, best not take it. She prides herself on her strawberry pie. Tastes like sugarless jello, but she'll tell you everyone loves it. Her best customer is old man Mort Hudson. Calls on her about every day for a free handout. He's got a shack somewhere near the falls, but don't know's anyone ever goes near it. I sure as hell wouldn't, not the way he smells. But you don't wanna hear gossip. The water works comes up next. Although there's some private wells and septic tanks in the less built-up areas, the water district supplies water from a common well to most residents."

Astrid wondered if they were real residents. She looked up at the water tower and thought it remarkable. On the farm an artesian driller had gone so deep that everyone had begun to think there was no water there. But the woman diviner said they would get it and to just keep drilling. She was right. They found an endless supply of clear, cold water.

Charlie began, "How about the…"

"I know what you're gonna ask. How about sewage. Well, again, they's a sewage plant on the other side of the island. Now, ahead is the cemetery and church where the minister I was just speaking of preaches. You'll note how well the church and cemetery are kept up. That's all thanks to the Society for the Preservation of Seaview Church and Cemetrery. It's a hard-working group and they raise a lot of money every year to keep up appearances. It's the heart of the island community, this church. Don't pay the minister much, though. There's priorities for ya. Can't blame the padre for not strainin' to create some new messages."

Just beyond the black-streaked headstones was the white church with three plain windows on each side, a spiral steeple and black roof shingles. Gently rising steps led to the double front doors. A straight and recently painted white fence separated church and cemetery.

"We're headed to the end of the island where less *worthy* residents--mostly fishermen, lobstermen, and carpenters--live. They're the island slaves, so to speak, to you gentler folk."

Rude man. Astrid felt like whacking the back of his head.

"The church at our end has weathered bad and the cemetery's been vandalized a few times by rambunctious teens, mostly at Halloween. Up ahead is the K through 12 school, the only school on the island and some kids have to walk for miles to get there. But they get a good education. We've produced college graduates who've become successful. Some of them retire to the island and either fix up their old family homes or buy classy ones at the rich end of the island. In case you from away haven't been told, that end is called Blue Haven. I don't know how it got that name, but that's it."

They were a distance from the water now, along a stretch of road with ordinary looking homes, well-tended gardens and pine trees. All at once she saw something else.

"The inland lake," she said. "That's where the loon lives."

Jeremy looked at her in his rear view mirror.

"We have a couple good-sized bodies of fresh water. They all have loons. So does the bay."

He continued his roller coaster inflection telling about the points of interest in the area while driving no more than 25 miles an hour, but Astrid tuned him out. The name Miriam resounded in her head, just like it did last night after she heard the loon's cry on the wind. A loon? Could it have been something else? She shook her head. Poor Miriam. Finding her now would likely be impossible, but she hoped Abram would have good news tonight when they talked. How could it be, though? Apparently no one could identify the car or its driver, so obviously finding someone who knew anything about the abduction was practically out of the question.

Maybe she should return to Fairchance and help in some way. But what could she do that they weren't already doing? That would be Abram's question if she mentioned returning. She could hear him now. *Stay where you are, Honey. You need to relax and enjoy yourself. Leave the sleuthing to us.*

Of course that's what he'd say. And he probably would mention the times she had found herself in a life or death situation because she got caught up in a tangle of mystery. It was an unfair judgment, really. After all, each time she became a victim herself, she was instrumental in bringing someone to justice. He knew that and so did Sheriff Larry Knight.

The abductors had nothing for the girl—no clothing, no hygienic items. They'd have to find these things at a store somewhere. Maybe they'd go to more than one store. And they'd want to keep from being noticed. So how would they accomplish that? She wondered if Abram had thought about checking stores in the countryside beyond that area. On the other hand, it might be safer for them to go into a busier city to shop for her special needs. Of course, the younger sister said she saw a woman at the wheel, so perhaps they'd just let that woman's things suffice for Miriam. That is, if they planned to keep her healthy--if they didn't plan to do away with her.

What a dreadful thought. They must find her. It was more frustrating than ever. Astrid yearned to look everywhere, check any plausible place for a clue. Maybe Miriam had a health problem, needed a special medication. But, of course, Abram and Larry and the other investigators would think of those things. If she ever thought she had answers nobody else would have, the reality was that she didn't.

Riding from one end of the island to the other somehow inspired little excitement for her, not at all like getting into fact-finding in a murder case. She hated to admit it, but she was bored.

She mustn't let it show. True, the homes were beautiful and big, but island life had to be terribly confining. How did people live here year-round? Winters must be about as pleasant as being in an igloo at the North Pole. She'd be grunting unintelligible phrases after a while if she had to face northeast storms here. The only thing missing would be the nearly 24 hours of darkness to balance out the solitude of it all.

That thought brought her back to the guide's words. He was saying "…and as you see we're now going through the town proper. On the left are the town hall, the health clinic, the mini mall where you'll find a florist, beauty saloon, real estate office, a dress shop, and a restaurant. That's our movie theayter next. It's one of the prettiest you'll find anywheres. Been there for a good many years, complete with gilt trim and velvet seats, and has been kept as bright as ever all those years."

His pronunciations amused Astrid, even though he himself annoyed her. Maybe it really was a beauty saloon--a shampoo and cut and a drink to go. She'd heard others say theayter. Still it was funny.

"Observe the mansion on the right where two of our town attorneys and an accounting office are now located. Once it was the home of the island's richest and most generous benefactor to Twilight Isle residents. He insisted that someone be hired to coach basketball and baseball competitive teams and then he had the gymnasium and ball field built. You'll see them as we go along."

From the back, Charlie called out.

"I'll hazard a guess that the man's name was Wingate."

Jeremy Barrett chuckled.

"Guess you noticed that we're circling the island on Wingate Drive, and the name over the mall entrance is Wingate, and here we are at the Wingate Sports Arena. Yup. You got it right. The first settler here was Captain Simon Wingate, and now his great-great-grandsons Garvin, Peter, and Grover Wingate carry on the family tradition of philanthropy. They're just plain folk, too, and we all respect and love 'em. People sometimes ask why ain't the island called Wingate Isle. Well, as I been told, the original Mrs. Wingate gave birth to three children on this wilderness island. You could say she ruled the roost, and when her husband said the island would be called Wingate Isle, she put her foot down and started packing up herself and the children to leave. That's how heated the discussion had become. She said it would be Twilight Isle or she was leaving to live with her parents on the mainland. Well, she never left."

Astrid laughed along with the others. Sometimes a woman just had to put her foot down.

"Now we're coming to the pride of the community, the Wingate Firehouse. A brand new ladder truck, three trucks in all, and full-time paid fire fighters."

"Do you have that many fires?" Dee asked.

"These houses are all wood and many of 'em burn wood in fireplaces or just plain old woodstoves. We get a lot of fires, and the firemen try to save homes as much as possible. They's a branch station on the other side of the island, but they's only a handful of volunteers there."

"I haven't noticed any burned-out houses," Jenny said.

"That's because if they burn, they get rebuilt or repaired in a jiffy. Island folk are family, so to speak. They gather for old-time building bees and keep things fixed up."

"That's generous enough," Jenny said in a barely audible voice.

Charlie asked, "How did the Wingates become so wealthy?"

"They was sea captains, traders. Sailing to China and back, carrying goods both ways. Yeah, made fortunes, they did. At least, those who survived the journey did. The coopulas you see on captains' mansions are called widows' walks. A wife would go up there and watch for her husband's ship to sail into home port about the time it was due. Many never did. But those that did brought home money and valuable goods. The Wingates were all lucky, fur as I know. They all come back and made fortunes. Lately younger ones don't take to the sea. You can be sure, whatever they turn a hand to's got money stuck on, though."

"They have the golden touch," Astrid said.

Helena added, "Money begets money."

"You saw the town hall we just passed," Barrett said. "When the island was settled, that and other gathering places were built on this end. It's closest to the ferry landing, and in those days there wan't no settlement at the other end. When the city folk discovered the island, they bought up land and built the big houses on that end. The settlers knew enough to stay on the protected end. It's like two separate towns, but the important buildings... school, town hall, and-so-forth-- remained over here." He looked at Helena and Eddie in the rear-view mirror. "You people have your own church and general store. Once in a while some of you join us when something appeals to you."

Wow, Astrid thought, *nothing like being direct and judgmental. Where'd they get this guy?*

Helena spoke up.

"I've found that we aren't always welcome in this neighborhood. But you're right. We don't try to mingle too often."

Astrid recognized the problem. Less well-off people were proud. She had felt that pride sometimes when wealthy buyers came to the farm and negotiated for horses. They apparently thought the unassuming appearance of the Phelps family and plain farm buildings meant they were poor, just people to patronize. How surprised they must have been to learn of the most successful franchise her grandfather established. Grampa took no guff from them, and they always left with a better understanding of how astute a businessman he was.

One thing she didn't believe, however. She wouldn't accept that Helena and Eddie were snobs. Like herself, they obviously were honest and fair with others. Well, *they* were honest. Astrid would have to admit that she was sometimes borderline honest.

As her thoughts rambled, the next thing she heard was, "This is it, folks, The Lobster Claw. All out. I'll be back by five. Enjoy your lobster."

CHAPTER 6

Outdoor one-piece picnic tables and benches, fireplaces with lobsters boiling in huge pots, and people wearing paper lobster bibs were not a new scene to Astrid. Any time she had driven downeast in summer she saw them next to salt water coves, at the edge of the highway. She had indulged in the delicacies herself. But the scene here seemed strangely out of place even though it was at water side. Where did all these people come from? All from the island? Or did mainlanders come over on the ferry to savor the atmosphere of lobsters on an island?

"Welcome to The Lobsta Claw, folks. Good to see ya, Mrs. Reese."

"And good to see you Lena" Helena said.

"I weren't shore when you'd get here, but lucky enough, we've lots of lobsta left. I'll take 'em out of the tank for boiling. Can't get fresher than that."

"No way. We're looking forward to the feast."

Lena's crooked smile lit up her leathery face. She took Helena's hand in a pump-handle shake. Astrid almost winced. That grip had to hurt, she thought. The hefty Lena had muscles that bulged like a man's. She wore bib overall and sleeveless white blouse, beneath a long rubber apron with bib top.

"Jus' follow me. We dug a hod o' clams in case you'd like some to go with your lobsta."

"No thanks," Helena said, after looking around to see if anyone wanted them. "Just the lobsters will do. And some fries."

"We got a good crowd for seafood today. Tourists flock here as much as the gulls do. I guess they feel like they're regula' pioneers comin' to a rough place like this,"

"It's a good place to have an outing. I don't think I've ever seen so many seagulls, though."

Jenny surveyed the sky and the several families around at picnic tables. She looked worried.

"Will the gulls bother us while we eat?"

Lena exploded into a loud belly laugh. Astrid thought the question appropriate given the hordes of squawking birds circling over the shore flats.

"You know what them gulls is doin'? At low tide, mussels show up on the rocks and gulls dive for 'em, then go up high, and drop 'em on the rocks. That opens the shells up so the birds can swoop down and pick up their snack."

She laughed again. "Pretty cleva, huh?"

"Pretty clever, indeed," Astrid said. "So they don't swarm around like that when the tide's high?"

"Not so bad, unless we throw out some old bait. They get some greedy then and ain't a bit polite to all the otha birds that sneak in for their share."

"They'll leave us alone while we eat, then."

"See any over the tables there? I don't think they'll treat you any different. They're pretty democratic."

"This is hard work," Charlie said.

Astrid hadn't seen him as enthused as he seemed today. His eyes gleamed as if he were a boy who had just seen an elephant for the first time at a circus.

"I helped a fisherman one summer as a teenager," he said. "Your husband out hauling traps is he?"

Lena looked like he'd just slapped her in the face, not so much shocked as hurt. Charlie turned around to face the water when she answered in a subdued voice.

"He died last winter. Fell overboard. They neva did get his body."

"Oh God. I'm sorry."

"Nevah mind. It goes with the job. All lobstamen know it could be them any day, 'specially in winta when they have to go way out to the deepest water. He knew the danger. Fall overboard and you're dead within five minutes if you don't get hauled out. Either freeze or drown or both. I told him not to go out that day. It was too windy and too cold, but the dumned fool had to do it his way. Nevah listened to me. Men nevah listen. They act like we know nothin' until they get sick. Then we're their angels and they turn into babies."

Lena's weathered face tightened. If anyone didn't understand her grief, they'd think she hated her husband. But Astrid understood. For a long time her own father blamed his wife for dying, even though she had pneumonia and was just too worn out from hard work to fight it. He said she shouldn't have walked to the neighbor's house on a bitter-cold day to take eggs and ham to the family of eight children.

"Me and my oldest boy carry on the lobst'rin' now, and my other boy Philip and his wife take care of the business end of it and the concession stand."

Helena and Eddie linked hands and followed Lena to the tank where the lively crustaceans crawled over each other. Astrid beckoned to Dee and Marvin as well as Charlie and Jenny to follow.

"Seven of ye. Okay. We have that many one-pounders."

"I guess six will do," Marvin said. "My wife doesn't like lobster."

The withering look Lena gave Dee said, *Doesn't like lobster? What's wrong with her?*

They all watched while she pulled the squirming creatures from cold water and promptly dumped them into a pot of boiling water.

"Fifteen minutes. I'll get the fries ready. Get a bib and tools from Philip at the counter. He has drinks, chips and cookies for sale. You can pay him for all of it."

She weighed each lobster and told Helena the total price. She glanced at the counter.

"Now, where'd he go to? I turn my back and he's out behind the woodshed dubbin' around on that old canoe. I don't know what fur. Can't use it in these waters, and snow'll be flying before he can take time off. No time then to use it in a river. He's a bit queeah at time, just like his pa. Can't tell him nothin', either."

Philip turned the corner just then, in time to serve the guests and take their money. The time went quickly after steaming lobsters were taken from the pot and delivered to the table. No one needed instruction in cracking the hard claws with a nutcracker, digging out the pink and white meat with nut picks and dipping it into melted butter.

"What a feast," Marvin said.

He nudged Dee's arm and grinned. While all the others wiped butter from their chins, she ate a sandwich that she brought with her.

"You don't know what you're missing, dear," he said. "Don't you want to try a bite of mine?"

"No, really. I don't want to get ill."

She pulled away as if it were poison. He shook his head.

"Have you always disliked seafood?" he asked.

"Never liked lobster or scallops. I became sick trying to eat them as a child, and never have liked them since."

Having no extreme dislikes in food, Astrid still would rather be at the kitchen table with soft music playing and Abram at her side than on this hard picnic bench swathed in that special odor of clam flats. She would relish a long, warm shower tonight.

Quiet, smiling Jenny looked up at her husband and said, "This is fun. Quite a treat, indeed."

Oh damn. Always someone in the crowd with an upbeat, positive attitude to shake the foundations of a good self-pitying moment into oblivion.

"Ya," Astrid said. "A seaside picnic isn't our everyday fare, for sure."

She smiled to prove her sincerity. Her hosts were generous in every sense of the word. The least she could do was be grateful. When did this feeling of loss come over her and why? Abram was doing his duty and she should be relaxed, having a good time. Had they become so close that she couldn't bear to be away from him for a few days and nights?

"When we go back," Helena whispered in her ear, "we'll pass the road that leads to that mysterious light, I'm quite sure."

Side-by-side, she and Astrid had said very little to this point. Time to shake the blues.

"I hope so," Astrid said. "I'm still surprised that I'm the only one who has seen it."

"I think you're the only one with such keen powers of observation and a sense of the mysterious. Most likely none of us would have paid any attention even if we had seen it."

Astrid pulled a claw from the lobster body and, with a strong grip, cracked it open. Juice spattered Helena's face. She laughed while wiping the salty water away with her bib.

"I'm so sorry," Astrid said.

"Not to worry. Maybe I'll do as much for you. Goes with the territory."

Eddie leaned over to look at Astrid.

"She has good aim herself, Astrid. She spattered me twice already."

His strangely rhythmic and resonant voice intrigued Astrid. Maybe she would ask him if he was French, though this didn't seem like the right time to get into family history with either him or Helena.

Chatter rose when the lobsters were no more than a heap of red shells at each paper plate, and questions about the rest of the week became the topic. It was finally agreed that if the weather remained as pleasant tomorrow everyone would enjoy a boat ride around the islands.

Family groups started leaving. Children scattered about, running off their excess energy before starting for home.

Astrid wanted to ask Lena why so many lobster boats bobbed about at anchor farther out in the wide part of the bay instead of being out with lobstermen pulling traps, but Lena had disappeared. Floating like square houses on broad canoes, the boats must mean that the fleet was in.

A young girl, maybe six years old, screamed as she ran from her brother. She was fast enough to reach the dilapidated boathouse with its ragged, chewed-out underpinning, the result of years of decay in salt water. A motion to the right of the playful scene caught Astrid's eye, and she focused on a man in high boots, crushed hat, and what looked like fishing clothes. He stood in the shade of a fir tree at the edge of the shore. Though she couldn't see his face clearly, Astrid felt a chill of fear by his motionless fixation on the girl. She began to worry about the child's safety. Ready to go after the girl if she ran farther, Astrid heard the father call to the siblings. No need for action, then, but she waited to be sure that the man didn't still come out and grab the girl.

Astrid's premonition of danger still gripped her when the man disappeared into the woods. Perhaps she was just in such a silly state of fear over Miriam's abduction that it was all in her imagination, but she did think the man was too interested in that child.

Helena had been talking with Dee, and now turned to Astrid.

"Are you daydreaming?" she asked. "You look like you're in a trance."

"Oh. Did you speak to me?"

"I said the bus is here. Ready?"

"Ya, of course. I was just...wondering how they stack the lobster traps like that, all straight in even rows."

Helena looked at the traps and back at Astrid.

"Yes. It is fascinating, isn't it?"

Her words dripped with sarcasm, but Astrid pretended not to notice the raised eyebrows. If she said anything about the man and his attention to the young girl, Helena would probably say her imagination was at work again. Maybe it was. This island had some kind of weird effect on her, the effect of suspicion that nothing was as it seemed. Spoken words took on sinister meanings, a man standing and watching a girl at play filled her with apprehension, a light in a cabin at night propelled her into a passion for investigation like she'd never had before. Probably all innocent enough goings on, yet Astrid felt as if she needed to be cautious and ready to spring into action any minute.

The sun began to fade into the rising gray haze bringing nighttime damp, cool air. Astrid hoped the route back would not entail so much to see and hear about. She'd had quite enough of these island habits and eccentricities, and more than enough of riding in a hearse with a gossipy driver for a tour guide.

CHAPTER 7

At nine o'clock Astrid thought Abram should be home and resting, but the phone rang six times with no answer. She hung up, disgusted with Larry Knight for keeping his squad this late. If they were making progress, it would be one thing, but apparently they were not. Well, she'd try every 15 minutes. He'd get home sometime.

Feeling hungry after the lobster feast in the afternoon and only soup for supper, she headed for the kitchen to see what she could scrounge in the refrigerator. At the table were Helena, Eddie, Dee and Marvin, each making a hoagie.

"Astrid. Good. Come have a snack with us," Helena said.

"It looks more like a meal. That's what I came down for. Where are Charlie and Jenny?"

"They didn't come down," Dee said. "I rapped on their door and told them we were going to have a light lunch, but got no answer. Maybe they're out for a walk. I knew you would be on the phone with Abram."

"I've noticed how tired Charlie looks. He's been working very hard," Astrid said. Eyeing the food, "That looks real good."

"Make your own," Marvin said. "Cold drink or hot? We have lemonade and tea or coffee."

"I'll stay with water, thanks."

She put together ham, cheese, lettuce, and tomato.

"Rolls and everything are so fresh," Astrid said. "Did you shop again, Helena?"

"No. Our caretaker was feeling much better today and went out for new supplies."

Astrid picked up sandwich and water and headed for the door.

"It's hot in here. Think I'll go out and get some cool air."

"I'll join you," Helena said.

The others seemed content to eat at the kitchen table. The two women went to the open porch and set their plates on the picnic table.

"Wait," Helena said. "Let me wipe off the chair seats. They get dirty outside like this."

Finished, she asked, "Did you enjoy your day, Astrid?"

"Ya. I did. Very nice day. Nothing like fresh lobster. And fresh air, of course."

"I wondered about that because you seemed distracted."

"I guess I was, to tell the truth. I'm a bit worried about Abram and the investigation. He's working very late hours."

"Ye-es?"

The split in the word and her tone gave Astrid the idea that Helena might be asking if he was really on the investigation into the night.

"I trust Abram fully," Astrid tried not to show the disgust she felt over the question.

"Oh, I'm sure you do, my dear. And I didn't mean to imply that you shouldn't. I guess it really did sound that way. From what Dee has told me, Abram is a reliable man. She thinks you and he complement each other in so many ways, and if so, then he'd have to be a good, honest man."

Good save, Helena.

"He is. I guess I miss him too much. I didn't think I would, but we've been very close since we were married two years ago. Well, even before that. I took care of him in my home just after we met until he could work again."

"Why was that?"

"He worked at a hardware store and was doing handyman work as well. I thought I needed a handyman to repair the old house I had just bought—one of the original Sears pre-fab houses. Turned out that was a laugh. I saw his ad and called him to come over and look at the job. I didn't realize just how much upgrading needed to be done until he outlined work that would take a year."

She stopped to take a bite of her sandwich and then went on.

"Anyway, later he was helping at the store and the owner's kid, a young teenager, thought he'd have fun by dropping a box of tiles from the storage loft for Abram to catch. Not knowing what was in the box, he caught it and tore his rotator cuff...badly. Then Abram was out of work, no place to go really, no home or apartment, so I invited him to recuperate in my home. I fixed up a place in the living room where he could relax and sleep in an overstuffed recliner chair, and he stayed there for weeks."

Helena patted Astrid's hand where it rested on the table.

"Aren't you the one. Imagine. Taking care of a stranger like that. He must have a very honest face."

"I'm inclined to make snap judgments when I meet people, but I know better. Still, that's what I did. And ya, he does have an honest face. You would be much more sensible, I'm sure."

"Ha." The exclamation seemed to surprise Helena herself. "I'm far less sensible than you think. I've had my day, believe me."

Astrid jumped, startled by a loud blast from the bay.

"Don't be alarmed," Helena said. "It's a tugboat heading back to home berth in Twin Ports. They always blast a horn along here in case any small boats are ahead of them even on a moonlit night like this. They also like to signal us on the island."

"Guess I've never heard one so close. They travel at this time of night?"

"Oh yes. The captains know this bay like the backs of their hands."

"Twin Ports is where Dee is from."

"Yes. It's a lovely port city. I was there once. I understand she did own a mansion in the city, but now she just has a home in the country. Have you been there?"

"No. I grew up on a farm and didn't get to the seaside much. I have to admit it's beautiful. Kind of damp at night, though."

Helena laughed.

"It is that."

"So you plan a trip around the islands tomorrow?" Astrid knew this, but hoped plans might have changed.

"We are. Do I detect a bit of reluctance from you?"

"I'll go along with whatever everyone wants."

"But you'd rather not."

"You're putting me on the spot. I was hoping to take that walk to where I see the light at night."

"Well why don't we then. You and I. The rest can go on the boat ride. Have you been around the islands, by-the-way?"

"Yes. When I was a teen, a friend of mine took me with her family and we spent the day on the water. I had the worst sunburn I've ever had in my life, even though I was out in the sun working on the farm every day. It did surprise me to get that badly burned."

"Nothing like the sun on water to peel the hide off you. I'll go by your window tonight and take a look at that light. I think I know pretty much the area it's in. We can ride to that side of the island and get as close as possible, but then we'll have to hike some, I think."

"Will Eddie mind if you don't go with them?"

"No. Why should he? We've been married 43 years. We're quite accustomed to doing things and traveling on our own."

Maybe that was Astrid's problem. Abram and she hadn't done anything that kept them apart overnight before, except when she was in the hospital. She couldn't feel quite as free to roam as Helena did.

"You know, Astrid, I believe something else is bothering you. Missing someone isn't complex, and friends fill in the gap for a while. You have more bottled up inside. You're not depressed, I think, just being very introspective. Did you quarrel with Abram before you left?"

"No," Astrid said with a giggle. "We don't quarrel in anger… not much, anyway. No."

"Then what is it? I can sense an inner conflict."

She looked directly at Helena and saw the set jaw, a face lightly tracked by the march of time yet still beautiful, self-assured and defiant. To defy her or question her wisdom would be unthinkable.

But why did she feel she had the right to pry into someone else's life? What gave her the right? No one should be an open book. Grampa used to say, "Keep your own counsel. Be your own person."

This was the time to clam up. *But be calm about it.*

"There's nothing to worry about, Helena."

"I'm not worried, my dear. Just concerned. I want to see you alive, not deadly serious and sad from within. You're a strong person, I know. But if you let stress get to you, you soon won't be strong."

The nerve. Helena was just too much. *Be civil, Astrid.*

"How long have we been out here? I hope Abram isn't asleep by now. Gotta go and call. See you tomorrow morning, Helena."

Practically running, Astrid passed through the kitchen and barely said good-night to the others. When was it that she felt this weak and too well read by someone else? Mother. A very conservative and proud Swede, *Moder* pointed to every fault and weakness, every word spoken out of place. She put blame where it wasn't due. Said her daughter would always be a rough farmer, never a lady. She wanted her daughter to be dignified, someone she could be proud of, not a bully like the boys, not a roughneck.

The day *Moder* told her she might better have been born a boy was the day Astrid cried. It was the way she said it in snarling derision that hurt so badly. Didn't she love her daughter? That was the question that never was answered. It was Grampa who helped her become a better person and less self-conscious. He must have noticed that she shed no tears when her mother died.

Before even sitting down in the library, she dialed her home number. After two rings, Abram picked up.

"I'm so glad to hear your voice, Abram," she blurted. "It's so late."

"What's wrong? You sound upset. What is it?"

She cleared her throat and thought fast. Mustn't make him worry about her, and he would if he thought something was troubling her.

"No, I'm not upset. Just missing you. How is the case going? Any developments?"

"I'm happy to say there are. We have the couple that took Miriam."

"That's great."

"Yes and no."

"Miriam? You don't have her?"

"We don't know yet where she is. They're not talking."

"But you know they're the abductors?"

"They admitted that much. The postmaster's wife was out walking the dog and saw a green car. She remembered that description on the news and called the police and they let us know. They were at a bar. Larry thinks they may be in the business of grabbing young people and selling them."

Abram's sigh told her how stressed he was, how difficult it all was.

"Then she may be gone already," Astrid said.

"Possibly. We've been interrogating the couple separately for hours. If we learn that they are abducting girls and selling them we'll have to call the FBI."

"You need sleep. Did you eat?"

"Yeah. I picked up a hamburger and chips. I'm good."

"I'll say goodnight, then."

"Wait. What about your day?"

"It's hardly worth mentioning. Lobsters and a long island bus tour. Nothing special."

"Okay. Hope to see you soon."

"Me too. Love you."

He was gone before she finished and probably didn't even hear the last. So worn out. There never was any question that he'd put his all into a case, especially this one. If only she could help out, but here on the island it was impossible to do anything constructive for the investigation. If only she were in Fairchance, if for no more than to have supper ready for Abram when he finished these long days. She could probably do something else like call schools and find out if there had been any other missing young people around the area and beyond. She wasn't aware of any, and TV news would have reported anything like that in the state. But what if no one knew? What if girls who weren't particularly cared for went missing and nobody reported their disappearance.

"Oh stop it. That just couldn't happen." Astrid mumbled to herself as she walked the hallway to her back stairs. "Well, I suppose it might."

She knew a girl in fifth grade that no one paid attention to because she was a ward of the state and had been put on that dreadful farm. Poor thing. As far as she knew nobody bothered to inquire about the girl when she was gone from class one day and never returned. So maybe, just maybe similar disappearances happened and nobody cared enough to report them.

Once again, imagination seemed to have a grip on her, most likely due to the island's remoteness and a feeling of solitude. How did residents stand it?

One thing for sure. I'll never take up residence on an island. I'd be batty in a month.

She came to the porthole and stopped to peer at the light somewhere across the end of the island. She hadn't been there long before Helena, binoculars in hand, came toward her.

"Ah, ha," she said. "So you see the light, I expect."

"Ya. It's there. Come, take a look."

After Helena studied the light through the binoculars, Astrid asked, "Do you know where it is now?"

"I can't really tell. I think I know how to get there. Most likely the best way to go is by water instead of car. We'll take our skiff tomorrow and see if we can find the place."

Helena linked arms with Astrid and walked her to her door.

"I wonder if that could be the scavenger's place," she mused.

"The scavenger?" Astrid said.

"We call him the island scavenger. Our taxi driver mentioned him today—Mort Hudson. He goes around in his boat at night and picks up whatever he can find along the shore. Sometimes he goes onto private property and picks up things that are stored out back. He's been seen taking a wheelbarrow and a lawn chair that

I know about. He's been in court a couple of times, and had to pay at least one fine. The problem is that he gets away so fast he can't be caught in the act of theft. So proving that he didn't buy an item is hard to do."

"And he lives over there?"

"Yes. Light at night is difficult to pinpoint. Well, we can go take a look tomorrow."

"Good," Astrid said. "I can't wait."

"Goodnight. Sleep well."

Astrid sat in the rocker an hour before she felt sleepy enough to go to bed. Her mind jumped from the island to Abram's investigation and back again, over and over. What happened to Miriam? Did the couple kill her before they were caught? Would Larry and the deputies be able to get the truth out of them?

"Oh, Abram. How I wish I could help."

CHAPTER 8

A bram jumped to his feet and began to pace. Why didn't he tell her the truth? Tell her that he was so rattled the first time she called he couldn't bring himself to answer the phone? Worst of it was when he mustered up enough composure to talk on the second call, he lied to her.

The news likely wouldn't reach her for a couple of days. It would give him time enough to explain his deception. She might never trust him again, but the sight of that poor girl's body still made him feel sick, and he still couldn't bring himself to relive the shock. Maybe it was no excuse for telling Astrid that the couple hadn't revealed Miriam's whereabouts. It just seemed easier to sound hopeful that young girl was still alive, even if she might face a life of slavery. At least that would be better than what actually happened. How could he spoil Astrid's vacation with the horror of it all?

At the living room bay window, he stopped walking, leaned on the sill, and scanned the vast hillside woods flowing down to the cozy city of Fairchance where lights created a halo over the entire city. All at once his frustration, his anguish, his after-the-fact reality of the girl's suffering and intense fear festered into an outburst.

"Why did they have to torture her?"

The vivid memory rekindled anger he felt at first sight of her naked body, beaten, bloody and lifeless, left on the bare wood floor like so much garbage. Abram had turned away while Larry crouched down to inspect the body from head to toe as if he were a doctor making a physical exam. How could he be so indifferent? How many years of police work did it take? Is that what years of this work does to a person? Is that what's ahead?

Do I want to harden so much that I don't get sick at the sight of horrific scenes like that?

The question haunted him, and probably would for many days and nights, maybe years. It's something he would need to discuss with Astrid. She'd probably give him some good advice. If she were here they'd have that discussion now.

Astrid. How can I tell you? How can I even discuss how I feel? How can I say to you that I saw my dear little sister there on the floor and that I wanted to go back to the cell and beat the hell out of both those monsters?

Should he call her back and tell her now? Could he even get her? She said there was only one phone in the house. Would anyone hear it ring?

He began to shake. This shouldn't happen. He was a sheriff's deputy. He should act like one.

"Dammit. Stop it! Don't be a child."

Heading for the stairs, he stopped when the phone rang.

Is it Astrid? No, it couldn't be. She was going to bed.

He ran to the kitchen phone.

"Hello?"

"How're you doing, Abram?"

"Larry. Oh, I'm okay."

"You sound shaky."

"I'm just fine."

His grip on the phone table was almost painful. Calm down. The shaking will pass.

"We've identified the body. I didn't call you earlier because I saw how irritated you were. You needed time to sort it out. I know. I've been there."

Abram snorted. "Yeah, I guess when I slammed my fist against the wall you got a clue."

He flexed his right hand to ease the pain in the bruised knuckles.

Larry laughed. "Don't worry about it. Happens to all of us the first couple of times."

The first couple of times. I don't want more than this one.

"Have you talked with her parents yet?" Abram asked.

"No. It isn't Miriam, Abe."

No doubt Larry heard Abram's squeak when he fell backward onto a chair.

"She was a prostitute by the name of Lisa Smith. At least that's the name we have on file. Doubt it's right. She used to hang out in a local bar at the edge of town. She'd get men to buy her drinks and then invite them back to her place, that shack where we found her body. You noticed there wasn't much furniture, just a bed and some old chairs, besides the kitchen stuff. Police booked her a couple of times, so her fingerprints were on file. Still, she kept right on with her work, such as it was. I guess the last guy she had there didn't find her worth paying for and beat her up when she demanded money. At least that's the way I size it up."

"Then why did the Wards...?"

"I questioned them again. He knew about that prostitute. Probably had some dealings with her himself, if you ask me. But he says he didn't know we'd find her body there. He said he just wanted us to think that someone there had taken Miriam. He said he needed a rest from the questioning."

"So did he tell the truth? Did he say where she is?"

"He clammed up. I've brought in a couple of part-time deputies to keep on questioning him tonight. Hopefully they'll wear the two down, tire them out, and maybe we can get the truth."

"How much have you told the media?"

"Nothing yet. I didn't even tell Beth any more than that we found the abductors. Until we can give more details I don't want any reporters hanging around and harassing us."

"Then I guess I didn't lie to Astrid after all. I told her we still don't know where Miriam is."

He sighed in relief.

"Good. Is she having a good time on the island?"

"Said she was, but she didn't sound convincing. I think she'd like to be here. You know what I mean—the lure of the investigation."

"Thank God she isn't here. Beth hounds me enough. I wouldn't want Astrid on my tail, too. And you know what I mean."

Abram was finally able to laugh.

"Sure do."

"Get here before eight if you can, Abram. We should go over all that we have now and see what we're missing. I'm too tired to stay here any longer myself."

*****

Thursday morning Abram got out of bed at 6:30. He couldn't sleep any more, not that he'd slept much at all. After talking with Larry he realized he couldn't just quit, not now. In fact, he was desperate to know the truth, even if he had to see another body. As long as the one he viewed wasn't Miriam, there could be hope that she was still alive. He felt ashamed feeling this relief. That body had been a person, even if she was a prostitute. She had a life and a name. Lisa Smith. He should be more sympathetic to what she suffered. It shouldn't matter who or what she was.

He wished that were so—that he could feel just as outraged that she met a horrible end, just as if it had been the teenage girl. But his honest feeling couldn't be denied. She toyed with that danger when she went into the business of selling her body for men's pleasure. She chose her own destiny. Made her own bed as it were. But was it her choice? Maybe she just didn't know how else to survive. Maybe she had wanted to be as honorable as anyone else. Maybe extreme poverty or other circumstance forced her into selling herself. Whatever happened, it was an end that no one should meet.

While he made himself a light breakfast and ate it too fast, Abram considered various scenarios from the possibility that Lisa was from a wealthy family that disowned her for some reason to the possibility that she was divorced and that her husband had kicked her out of their home with nothing but one dress. By the time he left for the office he decided that he needed to find out more about the dead woman. He must reserve judgment until he knew more.

When he arrived at the parking lot between court house and sheriff's office, he saw Larry's official white car turning into his reserved space. He hurried over.

"Good timing," Larry said. "Looks like a bit of weather headed this way. Did you listen to the weather report, Abe?"

"No. I just ate and ran in order to get here early."

Abram had never seen him so weary. Ordinarily Larry was a natty dresser, his wavy brown hair well combed. This morning he couldn't have combed his hair at all, just showered and let it go in all directions. His light brown eyes were barely visible beneath droopy eyelids. If he slept at all, it could have been in his uniform trousers and beige shirt judging by the wrinkles. Abram couldn't resist a little dig.

"You look like something the cat dragged in," he said.

"Feel worse. I slept in a recliner so's not to disturb Beth. But I kept waking up and thinking about this case. Who knew it would produce a murdered woman? Wonder if the Wards knew about it all along, or maybe even murdered the woman themselves. I wouldn't put anything past that pair."

"I'm with you there."

They climbed the four steps to the heavy front doors, where Abram grasped Larry's arm.

"I want to ask you. Did you find any money in that woman's house? I didn't see any."

"No. We searched it thoroughly, but none was found. Not a penny."

"Odd, isn't it? Don't prostitutes usually have a stash of money hidden somewhere? That came up in one of my classes, I remember. The prof said prostitutes always want to have enough money to get out, so they hide their money because they don't trust banks. They want to have cash on hand in case they need to move in a hurry."

"You're right. I didn't give it much thought. Just figured the killing was all about money, so the killer took what she had."

"What if he didn't? What if he just didn't find it, any more than we did? Her handbag was empty, yes. But I bet she had more, somewhere."

Larry pulled a door open.

"Let's talk inside. I need coffee."

Their steps echoed in the vacant hallway to the lounge where coffee had been made by one of the deputies. Sitting at the table to eat a doughnut with his coffee, Larry sighed as if he had taken a ton off his feet.

"So what are you thinking, Abram?"

"I'm thinking that if she had money hidden really well, she might also have other things hidden with it."

"Which could be significant."

"Well, you never know. I just think I'd like to go out there and do a more thorough search. I wasn't good for much yesterday."

"You can say that again. Okay. Let's talk to the night deputies first and find out if either of the Wards cooperated."

As Abram expected, the Wards had remained mum, though their interrogators kept up the questions most of the night. Mrs. Ward, being questioned in a room separate from her husband, simply slumped over the table in a dead sleep. Her husband was more tenacious, often grinning, sometimes mocking, but never giving anything away beyond what he'd already divulged.

Larry agreed that Abram might better spend his time doing the search than trying to pry information from the two.

Relieved to leave that aggravation behind, Abram was soon at the little house of horror, where he took time to look at what he couldn't yesterday...the blood stain and chalk outline of the slender body. Perhaps he could get used to this grisly business after all. He'd like to think so. In many ways his work satisfied the need to help people, a need he had recognized for a very long time before he met Astrid. If she hadn't urged him to go back to school, however, he might not be a deputy today.

"Thank God for Astrid. For so very much."

He couldn't shake the thought that this house had some connection to the abduction and that it was just possible the Wards pointed them in the right direction after all. They seemed genuinely surprised when they were told a body had been found here.

He recalled tips the professor had given the class about investigating this type of scene. In particular, he emphasized that the hideaway space had to be easily accessible for the one using it, but so unique that the average person wouldn't notice or find it on quick inspection. He told of one case in which loot was tucked away in the space between a stove firebox and the chimney—the flat space over the oven.

Not wanting to get too sooty at the beginning, Abram began by rapping the walls up and down, then stomping on the floorboards. He couldn't find a hollow space. Next came the ceiling, like everything else, dirty and cobwebby. Anyone hiding money in it would definitely leave fingerprints. None showed. Now he was stumped. The chairs had been well searched. He had watched the other two deputies check them.

"Where did you put it?"

Perhaps the kitchen would have a hidden space. Odd that there was no dresser for underwear and other things a woman would put away, he thought. It didn't take long to find that she used a kitchen drawer for her personal things, which amounted to very little. He went into the bathroom, no more than a toilet and small sink with a single faucet.

Obviously no place here to hide a hairpin.

When opened, the door barely missed hitting the sink. The flat riser under the door appeared solid, but he knelt to test it anyway. It didn't move until he placed his fingers on each side and pulled upward. He toppled over backward when it popped up.

"Well, looky here."

Before him was an open box stuffed with bills, mostly tens and twenties. He jiggled the box and found that it moved. Of course, she'd want to be able to get it out. So how...?

"Ah, yes."

On each end was a thin nylon string. He pulled the two ends. They extended to longer strings and he slid the box out with ease.

"That's clever."

Abram took it to the kitchen table where he could check the contents more thoroughly. As he dug into it, he found a red book like a diary with names written on several pages. Some were followed by telephone numbers and dollar amounts.

"Well, well, lady, you were a busy one."

Rather than count the money here, he wrapped a worn towel around the box, tucked it under his arm, and returned to the sheriff's office. Larry was gone, probably still with the honored guests in the basement. Abram sat at Larry's desk to study the red book. He took his time, hoping to find a clue. Maybe someone who had paid her a few large sums suddenly stopped visiting or lowered his payment. It could be a way of recognizing a problem. But would it be enough of a disagreement or dissatisfaction to build up a murderous anger?

Then he saw what he'd overlooked on quick glance.

"Hello. What's this?"

"What's what?" Larry's voice startled him. "Looks like you found the stash. Good for you."

"And something else," Abram said. "A little red book of clients' names and what they paid for services. At least she wrote some amounts in. But I just found something else. What do you make of this?"

He left the book open and stood up so Larry could have his own chair.

"Right there." He pointed. "See what I mean?"

"Yeah. I see. But I don't know what to make of it. Looks like code for something in addition to her nighttime job."

Larry flipped pages.

"There are at least four of these codes. Initials and numbers that look like they could be dates."

Aloud, he read the initials, page by page, writing them on a notepad as he did: 1GB-6-5-92, 1GH-6-8-92, IGB-6-12-92, 1GB-7-1-92.

"You know what, Abe? She had something else going, something more important. I'd say it was important enough that she tried to keep record, while not making it clear if someone discovered the box."

"Another thing, Larry. When I studied the murder scene, it struck me that there wasn't much blood around, even though the body was drenched in it."

"You're right. We had determined that. Someone beat her to death somewhere else and then deposited the body at that house. I don't think the Wards are the killers. But it's probable that they knew the woman."

Abram stared at three pictures of antique Fords gracing the end wall, and asked, "You ever have anything like this before, Larry?"

"Never. And it has me stumped. I'm coming up blank. Now that we have this diary maybe we can get somewhere. She had business nearly every night of the week. No wonder she was thin as a rail. Interesting list, huh? We'll have to talk to all of them. Look at this one. Our honorable Mayor Demetrie. He made a regular Wednesday evening visit. Cheapskate, though. Paid only ten bucks. Some of these guys paid twenty-five. Surprising she didn't set a standard price, don't you think?"

Abram sank into deep thought about the code and what the initials meant. However, he heard the last question and nodded.

"Now, all we have to do is decipher the code letters," Larry said.

Hunching his shoulders, Abram said with a yawn, "Piece of cake, I'd say."

CHAPTER 9

Astrid had been on the island two days and here it was Thursday morning and she still didn't know any more about the light she saw each night. She didn't intend to let this day go by without taking a look at where it came from. Why was it the only one visible in that area, the one no one seemed to know or care about? Well she did. There must be something of interest on this chunk of land in the middle of a very large bay. Lobsters, clams, fresh fish, and seagulls might be enough for the others, but without Abram it all seemed like a useless waste of time. Even touring the islands by water didn't spark her interest. But the phantom light did. It might be nothing to bother with, nothing more than a timed light someone had in a small shack. Imagine that. But for some reason it drew her like a magnet each time she looked at it. She felt as if time were running out with a life at stake, and that seemed just ridiculous. It certainly wasn't anything she'd say out loud to anyone, not even Helena.

"Oh dear."

The last time she felt this intuition she was nearly killed.

While all but Helena assembled for breakfast and ate waffles, scrambled eggs and bacon, Astrid observed how relaxed they were, not tense like they were at the newspaper office. Everyone had overslept. This had to be a good vacation idea and she knew it. They had all needed a change of scene. That was the truth of the matter, but relaxation wasn't her best endeavor.

Why am I creating a scenario that will turn out to be nothing more than a fantasy in my silly head?

Doubt threatened to take over when she thought of what Abram would say if she started climbing around a rugged shoreline and got hurt. But last night at about 2 a.m. she tiptoed to the window and looked again. The light appeared larger and brighter than ever among humps of dark rock and trees barely outlined under a moonless sky.

Why didn't Helena come down? Maybe the day *was* overcast, but still they could take a spin around that section just to see what was there. Finally she called down the table.

"Is Helena coming down, Eddie?" she asked.

"She had a restless night. I told her to sleep a bit longer this morning."

"I hope she's okay."

"Seems to be. Just a combination of fresh air and rich eating, I'd say. It's a little too much. She's tired."

"Are we still on for the boat tour?" Charlie said. "Weather report on the radio was that a cold front is moving in fast and it will bring wind and rain."

Eddie got up, went to the sink window. He peered one way and the other. When he turned around, he looked worried.

"It's hard to tell right now," he said. "But I don't like the sight of those black clouds over the mountains. Could be a northeaster coming in. If so, we don't want to be out there. When winds back up in a counterclockwise direction around the Gulf of Maine in a northeaster, anyone out in a boat could face a life threatening struggle."

"Is that likely at this time of year, you think?" Jenny said.

Charlie scowled at her.

"If he knew that, he'd tell us, Jen. I think he's saying we'd better wait a while and see what develops."

Astrid wished Charlie wouldn't always correct his wife in that superior tone, especially in front of others. Abram didn't do that. If he had a bone to pick or wanted to set her straight about something, he'd wait until they were alone.

What am I thinking? Charlie is a good husband, too. Gotta stop judging others.

"*Oui*," Eddie's unusual use of French was a surprise. Astrid hadn't heard him speak the language before. "We'll soon know. If it doesn't start to rain, we'll have lots of time to go out."

Breakfast was nearly over when a woman in white Bermudas and black cotton shirt came through the back door carrying an over-the-shoulder bag.

"What is it, Millie?" Eddie said.

"Mail, sir. I forgot to deliver it yesterday. Still a bit under the weather, you know. Sorry."

"That's okay. Mostly bills, no doubt. Feeling better, are you?"

"Oh yes. That's a helluva flu bug goin' around. Hope none of you get it. Missus feeling poorly?"

"No, just sleeping in."

"I'll take hers up to her. Sky is sure dark out there."

Millie likely had been with the family for years, judging from her forward way of speaking and her readiness to go to Helena's room without so much as asking permission. Astrid noted that Eddie paid no attention, just flipped through a half dozen envelopes and set them aside on the counter.

While everyone lingered over coffee, Astrid tried to think what she could do for the day if they didn't go out for the boat tour. After planning with Helena to take a small boat over to the area of the light, she'd be more down in the dumps than ever if they didn't make it. There must be something a little more exciting than riding around the bay in a yacht or possibly sitting out a storm in the library trying to read a book. Concentration seemed impossible lately. A little adventure would certainly perk her up.

"Do you think Helena would mind if I went to her room to speak with her, Eddie?"

"Of course not. Go on up. She's probably just reading ads in the mail."

Dee said under her breath as Astrid walked by, "Never saw you so restless."

Astrid shrugged and moved on, to the front foyer, up the winding stairway, and down the hallway to the end suite. She rapped on the door.

"It's Astrid. Are you okay?"

"Astrid. Yes, I'm fine. Come in."

Helena was dressed in a light blue pants suit.

"You're going somewhere?"

"I have to go into town. Some bank business that I must attend to. So sorry, Astrid. I know you had your heart set on investigating that light. But we can do it tomorrow."

"Might not have been able to go today, anyway. They say a storm appears to be brewing. I guess I'll find something else to do. Just wanted to touch base with you."

"You're like a fish out of water, my dear. Do you think you want to stay here or would you rather go back to Fairchance?"

Astrid looked away, pretending to study the weather out the side window. Everyone must be able to see through her. It was embarrassing and she felt like a small child, homesick and moping around. She had to snap out of it.

"Oh no. I didn't realize that I was making a spectacle of myself." She smiled but knew it was unconvincing. "There are some good books in the library. If we can't go out, I'll be perfectly okay. Well,

I'll leave you to finish getting ready to go to town. Will the ferry still run if the weather's bad?"

"It has to get really bad before it stops running. If I get caught on the other side in a big storm, I know a woman who will put me up for a night."

"Oh. That's good."

Astrid opened the door and looked back at Helena.

"Have a good one," she said.

Now she felt even more like a child trying to sound cheerful and off-hand about being left alone while Mother went off to work somewhere.

"Don't look so down-hearted, Astrid. If you'd like to go with me, you're welcome."

The invitation sounded insincere. Astrid wanted to say she'd be happy to go along, but shook her head.

"No, no. You have business to tend to. I'll be just fine. See you later."

She hurried out the door and down the hall, trying to control all the emotion that flooded through her and hating this feeling of being trapped. It must be the island. She had no Jeep to hop into and drive away, didn't much care about boating, couldn't very well take a walk outside with rain probable. This must be what being in jail felt like. If she could just pick up the phone and talk with Abram. But he was busy doing something worthwhile, unlike her.

This just will not do. Get a grip, you idiot. This isn't the end of the world, you know. You've been alone before. You were alone long before you met Abram. Why so depressed now? He's okay. You're okay. The world's okay. Buck up.

She squared her shoulders, took a deep breath, and practiced smiling, ready to join the others in the kitchen.

"She's about ready to leave for the ferry," she announced while pouring another cup of coffee.

Eddie entered through the outside door, his face red and hair rumpled.

Smoothing back his thick white hair, he said, "It's getting windy. I'm afraid we *are* due for that storm. Why is she leaving?"

Helena heard the last as she walked toward him from the back hallway.

"The bank sent me a notice to see them immediately, dear. I'll be all right. Don't worry. This business is important. I'll tell you about it when I get back."

"I don't know..."

Her kiss interrupted his objection. Astrid could see how the wind blew in their relationship. Helena had made up her mind to go and would hear no more about it.

"See you this afternoon. 'Bye all."

And she was gone.

"How will she get to the ferry?" Marvin asked. "Does she drive herself?"

Dee reached for his hand, obviously telling him not to offer to drive Helena.

"Yes, she can drive. She usually does," Eddie said.

If ever a man looked and sounded more distressed over his wife's action, Astrid had never seen one. Eddie repeatedly ran his hand through his hair and paced to the window, back to the table, and back to the window.

"It's beginning to rain," he said.

Astrid would have said it was beginning to pour oil over the glass. The heavy downpour quickly darkened the room. Gloom invaded the room as wind roared, pounded against windows and banged against the building. The darker and louder the storm, the quieter everyone became. Astrid shivered. Why did Helena find it necessary to head out in a storm that she must have known from experience would strike with force? Seemed like she could have called the bank and told them she'd be there when the weather was better.

Staring sad-eyed at the rain shards against the glass, Eddie half whispered, "Colder and louder blew the wind, A gale from the Northeast."

Astrid started, surprised that a Frenchman could quote from Longfellow's work.

"That's ominous, considering what happened to the *Hesperus*," she said.

Eddie drew a deep breath and let it out slowly. Once again he returned to the table, this time to sit beside her. He appeared ten years older than when breakfast began. Threads of wrinkles had become ropes of worry, pulling at his mouth and eyelids.

"It is a poem that has haunted me ever since I first read it. Though the sea looks beautiful in the distance, it can be a cruel vixen, ready to torture the unfortunate person who doesn't respect its wrath and power in a strong gale."

A streak of light flashed, followed by the roll of thunder.

"Are you afraid of these storms?" Astrid asked.

"I fear what they can do, yes."

"Sounds like you've had a bad experience."

His head snapped up when the room lit up in another bright flash. The boom sounded like it would crash through the ceiling. The others at the table yelled reactions from "That's a big one!" to "Sounds like it hit something nearby."

"I wish those people upstairs would quiet down," Charlie quipped.

So like Charlie to try to lighten the frightening air of pending doom.

Eddie looked at the door as if hoping Helena would enter through it.

"I had an experience bad enough to teach me the power of wind, rain, and lightning on the water. This isn't just a passing shower. It's a northeaster. Look. Sleet's pounding against the window."

"Not sleet," Marvin said. "It's hail."

He and Dee went to the back door to peer out.

"Look at the size of the stones," Dee said.

"They look like ping pong balls on the green grass. I've never seen a summer storm like this."

"You can see out?" Jenny asked.

"Barely."

Helena might be near the ferry by now.

"You think Helena will be all right?" Astrid asked Eddie. "Will the ferry run?"

"I don't think it will. If she can see the road well enough to drive back, I'm sure that's what she'll try to do."

This was scary, just a bit more tension than Astrid had expected. If she had gone with Helena, there wouldn't be anything she could do except hope that the car stayed on the road. Now she wished she hadn't left the Jeep for Abram to use.

"Is there any place near the ferry that she can find shelter?"

The look of terror that crossed Eddie's face made Astrid wish she hadn't said that. Why was he so frightened?

"I…" His voice broke and he coughed to cover it. "I think Mr. and Mrs. Johnson are on the island now. They live a block from the ferry. They'll take everyone in if they can't get across."

Thunder exploded after each lightning fireworks display.

"I don't like coming here, but Helena enjoys it so much I can't refuse."

It was as if Eddie were talking to himself. He was quiet a good five minutes while the whining storm shook the house with a demonic life of its own. No one spoke. If they had said anything, they likely wouldn't have been heard.

Eddie's fist slammed the table top, rattling dishes as well as nerves.

"She knows. She knows! But she always has her way. If anything happens to her today, I'll never forgive myself for not putting my foot down just once and keeping her home."

Why is he so weird? Does he think there's great danger for Helena at the ferry?

Without excusing himself, he left the room. Looks of alarm were exchanged before Dee broke the silence.

"What was that all about, Marvin?"

"I don't know. I've never seen him like this. When they visited our house, I always thought they were the calmest couple I knew. He sounded like he's terrified of storms."

"But you'd think she was going to the gallows the way he was carrying on!"

"Huh," Marvin laughed. "You have a way with words, my dear. But you're right. It did sound like she was facing death."

"Well, I don't know about all of you," Charlie said, "but I'm going to the library and get something to read. There aren't so many windows in there. Maybe it will seem less wild."

"I'll go, too, dear," Jenny said. "How about you, Astrid?"

"I think I'll go to my room for a few minutes. I'll be down later."

"What do you say, Dee?" Marvin asked.

"You go on in. Astrid, you want to wait a minute to give me a hand cleaning up the dishes and getting things in order out here first?"

Astrid had already begun to pick up dirty dishes and was placing them in the dishwasher, a luxury that she was surprised to find given the lack of some other modern conveniences here.

"Do you think something's wrong, Astrid? The way Eddie came apart. It looked like he knew something he wasn't telling us."

"That's what I was thinking. But Helena didn't have any qualms about going. I doubt there is anything to worry about."

She said it, but she didn't believe it. Looked to her like there was much to worry about. Eddie was normally a put-together man.

Everything cleaned up and dishwasher running, the two started toward the hallway door. They did an about face when the outside door banged open and the caretaker burst in, dripping wet.

"The ferry…!"

"What?" Dee's voice echoed his panic.

"The ferry," he yelled. "Got word on the ship-to-shore. There's been an accident. Where's Mr. Reese?"

The words were barely out of his mouth when the lights flickered off and the dishwasher stopped.

CHAPTER 10

Backing out of the parking lot, Abram glanced up at the darkening sky and briefly thought he should have listened to the weather forecast this morning. Never mind, doesn't matter. Larry had left, so he hadn't consulted on this. Abram knew he had to go back to the murder scene. Third time there. Should pretty well know the place inside and out by now.

No one ever accused me of being a quick study.

Rain clouded the windshield, and by the time he was at the one directional light in the middle of Main Street, lightning flashed.

Man alive! That was a big boom.

As thunder crashed, the drizzle all at once turned to a blinding flood. His decision to use the Jeep while Astrid was away served him well. He continued through the city at a slow rate. With low visibility, roads were virtually clear of traffic. But Abram couldn't take the time to stop and wait it out. It was important that he do this.

He found the dirt yard at the old house soft and slick. It would soon be mud at this rate. His truck would have gotten stuck, no doubt. He waited only seconds before pushing the door open against a powerful wind and dashed for the house. At least he'd had smarts enough to wear his rain jacket, but the slanting sleet left his legs feeling frozen in the few moments it took to get into the house. Rain pounded on the roof so hard that he looked out the window to see why it was so loud. The weather was changing by the second.

"Hail stones. In July, for crying out loud."

Thundering kettle drum rolls followed each streak of lightning. For a small house, it might be Usher's with its rocking, dark, wailing walls. A quick exit would suit Abram just fine.

I can do this.

When he searched the place before, he kicked something small that went under the stove. He didn't get down to see what it was then. Maybe it was nothing, but he had to know. He was looking for hidden money, and that certainly wasn't it. He didn't pay attention then, but in thinking about it, he decided he should give it another look just in case it was relevant to the case. The other officers didn't see it, but they weren't searching much around the stove, whereas he had taken off the stovetop covers and looked inside. However, he didn't feel around in the ashes. It was when he moved his position to see inside that his foot hit whatever went under the stove.

He found a worse-for-wear towel in the kitchen, straightened it on the floor to protect his knee, leaned down with his head almost touching the floor, and…yes. There it was. He needed a tool to extend his arm reach. The stove poker would do.

"Just the thing."

He knelt down again after taking the poker from a hanger on the side of the stove and ran it under the stove. Finding what he wanted, he pulled out what looked like a round pin.

"A Rotary lapel button. Who would've guessed."

Whoever carried in the body must have lost it from his lapel and either didn't notice or couldn't find it since it was just out of sight by the stove.

"So one of the killers is an upstanding Rotarian."

Careful not to smudge possible fingerprints, he picked up the wheel-shaped button with his gloved hand and bagged it, anxious to get back to the office. He opened the door to face the powerful wind again.

Little white stones covered the ground. He couldn't remember ever seeing hail stones in summer.

"Guess I'd better wait a few minutes. Wonder how long before it lets up."

As he waited, he wandered about the house, still looking for anything they might have missed. Shivering, he went to the bathroom to find another towel and wash his grimy hands. He reached for the soap.

"Yuk. What a mess," he mumbled when he felt the liquid build-up of soap. "Well, it's soap and I can rinse the stuff off."

He picked up what was left of the soap bar and with it came the top part of the metal dish, the part with holes. The dish below was nearly as messy as the top, but in it Abram saw something else. He dumped the dish in the sink.

A key. Another clue? It was no surprise that anyone searching the house would by-pass this mess. After wiping his hands and the key, Abram put it into another plastic bag and pocketed it with the Rotary button.

"I gotta get out of here."

He put his head down and ran to the Jeep, disregarding the needle sharp wind. At the office, he made another dash, up the stairs and down the hallway to Larry's office, not expecting to find him in already. But there he was, talking on the telephone.

Abram stepped back into the hall to wait for the click of the phone before going in and closing the door behind him. Generally the corridor was noisy with traffic. No need for anyone else to know of this.

"What is it, Abram?" Larry looked him up and down. "You look like a drowned cat. Is it that bad out there?"

"You didn't go out? I thought you were out when I left."

"No. Just checking the prisoners. You've got something?"

"Oh, not much, Larry. Only the possible identity of our murderer."

Larry's eyes widened in a question that said, "Go on," while he appeared to be at a loss for words.

Abram pulled a straight chair to the desk, where he placed the button for Larry to see.

"I went back to the house because I remembered kicking something when I searched before. It rolled under the stove and I forgot about it when I uncovered the box of cash. Then last night in bed, it came back to me. I never looked under the stove. So I did this morning, and I found it. Appears to be important."

Larry turned the Rotary wheel around to read it.

"I guess it is. He's not only a Rotarian. He's the treasurer as well."

Larry picked up his phone and dialed. Abram heard it ring twice.

"Conrad. This is Larry Knight," he said. "Fine, thanks...yeah, the baby's a big boy now. Say, I need a name. Your club treasurer."

Hearing it, he gave Abram a surprised look.

"Oh? Well...okay. No, nothing special. Just had an inquiry. Thanks Conrad."

"Well?"

"It seems that our mayor wears more than one hat, or should I say pin. Wouldn't be surprised if he does a little moonlighting on the side, too."

"The mayor?" Abram realized his mouth was open. "Nathan Demetrie? Well, I'll be..."

"Yeah, me too."

"His name was in the red book. What were they into? He had to have been in a mindless rage to pummel her like that. If he was the one who did it."

Larry picked up the red diary and flipped a few pages.

"Yup. The first sign of the coding was beside his name. Maybe that's when this mysterious activity started."

"Well," Abram said, "maybe we can find out what this key goes to."

"You found it at the house also?" Larry asked.

"It was in the soap dish."

"Somebody's head will roll for not finding these things when we searched."

"I can see why they wouldn't. It was a mess of old softened soap on top as well as in the lower half of the dish. Not something anyone wants to put his hands into. And I didn't see the pin until I accidentally kicked it under the stove."

"They should have found everything, anyway."

While Larry studied it, Abram asked, "You'll make an arrest, Larry?"

"We'll question him first. Come with me. We'll stop next door and get Chief Rawleigh. Doesn't matter how bad the weather is. We need to get that man."

"How about state police?"

"Let's see what develops before bringing them in. We may be barking up the wrong tree. Maybe the Rotary pin was lost in a regular Wednesday night rendezvous. If this turns into a major operation like some smuggling activity, it will be investigated by the FBI. But, like I just said, the mayor may be no more than pitifully embarrassed, instead of guilty of murder."

"Maybe."

But Abram had a gut feeling they had the killer.

"What did you say it's like out there now?" Larry asked.

"Wicked rough, but I think it's letting up."

Larry stood up and gathered what he needed.

"Can't let a bit of weather interfere."

After stopping for Police Chief Rawleigh, Larrry outlined what they had so far in the investigation as they rode to the mayor's house. In the back seat, Abram recognized the neighborhood they came to as one the most prestigious in Fairchance. Demetrie's mansion had always intrigued him when he passed it. Statuettes dotted the manicured lawns along with hedges and several round flower beds, all beaten down and dead-looking today.

They piled out of the patrol car, put their heads down, and ran for the shelter of the covered front walkway. Larry pressed the doorbell.

Chief Rawleigh let out a low whistle.

"Some digs. Must pay well to be mayor. Maybe I'll run for the job next election."

Pointing to the crepe on the door, Larry said, "Don't forget, they lost their son on the fourth. Be tactful."

Rawleigh said, "I know. It's still one helluva mansion."

When Larry mentioned the drowned son, Abram felt guilty about accusing the mayor of murder. Surely he couldn't have committed such a gruesome act with the tragedy of his drowned son on his mind. No one could be that callous.

The door was opened by a teenage girl in a too short mini-skirt. Abram focused on her thin face. It crossed his mind that her dark hair would soon reach the skirt hem if she continued to let it grow.

"Tracy, isn't it?" Larry said.

"Uh-huh. You want somethin'?"

"Is your dad home?"

"No."

"Do you know where he is?"

"No."

"Maybe when he'll be back?"

"Never, I guess." She shrugged. "I don't know much about his business."

"Well, may I speak with your mother?"

She turned away and yelled, "Mom. Some guys at the door for you."

Since the door was wide open, the three men went inside and closed it behind them. In a foyer large enough to be a living room, Abram looked around at white upholstered chairs and marble top tables beneath gold leaf mirrors, all against red walls. He had thought Astrid and he had an elegant home, but this topped all.

He looked up the circular staircase when a woman's faint voice said, "Sheriff Knight. If you're here about the funeral, there won't be any. We're having a memorial service for Billy next month."

"My apology for intruding at this time, Kay."

She got to their level, walked over, and gripped Larry's hand.

"It's all right, Larry. The worst is over," she said in a shaky voice. "Just look at all the flowers in the parlor. So many well-wishers. I believe there's a basket from you, too."

"Yes, I'm sure. Of course the townspeople share your sorrow for a young life lost so tragically. We'll stay here and only drip on this carpet, thanks. Sorry about that."

"Don't worry about it. That's made for all kinds of weather."

After questioning looks from Kay Demetrie, Larry said, "We're here to talk with Nathan. Is he home?"

"No. Is something wrong? Has he done something?"

Abram thought the answer came too quickly. And why would she necessarily think her husband had done something? As pitiful as she looked, he began to think something didn't smell right here.

"We're not sure yet. But if we can ask him a couple of questions, I'm sure he can shed light on the issue."

"On what? Maybe I can help."

"I'm afraid not. Where is he?"

She paled. At that question she touched her forehead, as white as the satin robe she wore, hand shaking. She pretended to brush back strands of mostly white hair. Perhaps it was the stringy white hair, or perhaps the thin lips drawn taut, or the guarded eyes. Mrs. Demetrie appeared to be a failing lady in her mid-sixties, though Abram was sure she was ten years younger. She pulled a heavy chair away from the wall and sat, as if she were in a faint.

"I don't know where he is. He goes away and tells me he's on a business trip. I didn't think he'd go this week, but he did, just as if nothing had happened. Just as if Billy would be here when he got back. I don't know."

As apparently weak and shaky as she was, Abram thought that if her husband turned out to be the killer she'd have to be stronger than this.

"Why couldn't he stay with me and Tracy? He knows she doesn't pay any attention to me. She comes in at all hours. Won't tell me where she's going or where she's been. Some of the characters she goes out with scare me. It's so hard."

The whining squeaks and heaving shoulders gave the impression of crying. Larry pulled a clean handkerchief from an inside pocket and held it out to her. She shook her head and dabbed at the tears with a lace hanky from her own pocket.

"He may be in Augusta. He seems to have a lot of business there."

She gave Larry a sideways glance, a quick look maybe to see if he was buying her story.

"Yes," she said. "I think he's probably there."

"Where might we find him in Augusta?" Chief Rawleigh asked.

"Why, I expect at some office that works with mayors like him. I know there is such an office, but I don't remember what it's called at the moment. I guess I'm just too distraught."

"Yes. No doubt. We'll leave you then," Larry said. "Will you be all right? Do you want someone to come over and help you? I have a maid who…"

"No. I have a maid and other workers here. It's just not the same. Not the same without my husband."

"No, of course not. If Nathan should come in, please let us know. You may call me at the office or at home, any time of day or night if you need anything."

"I will," she said.

Without saying more, they all left. To everyone's surprise, the sun was pushing away the storm.

Abram said, "A nor'easter one minute and clear sky the next. If this isn't the weirdest thing I ever saw, even in Maine."

Rawleigh said, "What do you think, Larry? She on the up and up?"

"My impression is that she's lying. She knows where he is alright. The question is can we find him."

Abram waited until he had time to think about what he'd observed. At last, he decided to comment, even if it was off the wall.

"I found it strange that Mrs. Demetrie wears no wedding ring. I'd expect to see a big diamond on her finger. Maybe it became tight and she had to take it off. Happens, I guess. But even odder to me is that she wears dress shoes—high heels at that—with her robe at home. Could mean nothing at all. Just seems odd."

"You don't miss much do you, Abe?" Larry said. "I didn't notice any of that, but if you saw that much, something could be fishy in Denmark. Are you thinking of something in particular?"

"Who knows? She going out to shop on a day like this? Hardly seems any woman would want a new dress that bad. Could be another man in her life, I suppose. If she knew about her husband's infidelity, she could have gone looking for greener pastures herself."

"I think you're onto something," Larry said. "Maybe she had just returned. It's a house divided there, for sure. Our priority right now is to find the mayor. I'll make a call to Augusta. She might be telling the truth." A long pause. "But I doubt it."

CHAPTER 11

W hen they returned, Abram continued on down the hallway past Larry's door since Larry asked Chief Rawleigh to come to his office. He thought Larry wished to discuss the case with the chief in private. However, he hadn't gone far before Larry called.

"You too, Abe." The only man Abram allowed to shorten his name was Larry Knight. "We'll all go over what we have so far."

"You want me?"

"You've done more than anyone else toward solving this mess, Abe. You better continue on with us."

Abram tried not to strut, but he felt honored by that. After all, he was only a deputy, and pretty much the last one hired at that. It meant that he'd done a good enough job to earn respect from his superior. Couldn't ask for more than that.

The meeting of the three men went on for 20 minutes before Larry picked up the key that Abram found. He showed it to the chief.

"Any idea what it's for? It's not a house key, and not at all like a safe deposit box key. I can't figure it out."

As he said that, Julianne, the dispatcher on duty today, came in without knocking. Abram would never have done that when he was acting as a dispatcher, but Julianne was a bit on the rough side. She really would make a good deputy, he thought.

"I have a report for you, Larry."

"Okay. Just leave it here on my desk."

She nodded to Abram and the chief as she approached, put the report down, and saw what Larry held in his hand. She had heard him talking about it when she came in.

"I know what that is," she said. "It's a boat key. My dad has a pleasure boat and he uses a key just like that."

"Well, thank you, Julianne."

"Sure." She left as quickly as she arrived.

Larry looked from one to the other.

"A boat key," he said. "At least we know that we're looking for someone along the coast. Without the key, the boat should still be in one of the harbors."

"Where's the nearest fishing harbor?" Rawleigh asked.

"Twin Ports," Abram offered.

"That's what I'd say," Larry said. "This is not the day to go looking. I'll call the harbor master. Maybe they can give us a clue as to what we're looking for. I sure as hell don't know."

"Why do you suppose Lisa Smith hid the key?" Abram wondered aloud.

"Maybe it was her boat, and she planned to get away in it," Rawleigh said.

Larry thought a minute before giving his opinion.

"A boat costs a lot of money. She had a stash, but I doubt she had enough beyond that to buy a boat. More likely it was someone else's and she was either keeping the key for blackmail or had stolen it."

Abram could think of nothing to offer. Why did Lisa need to hide the key? The whole case was baffling. If the mayor were the killer, did the key play a significant role? Maybe he didn't do it. Maybe someone else was involved and…well, he couldn't get his thoughts together to look at other scenarios, so he stood and headed for the door.

"You're leaving?" Larry asked.

"Thought I'd do that calling for you. I can find out about the registered boats in the harbor and if one belongs to Nathan Demetrie, it'll save some time."

"Good idea."

From what dealing he had with Police Chief Pat Rawleigh, Abram had concluded that the man's deductive powers were lacking. Larry, on the other hand, had a track record of making sound judgments in his cases. No doubt he was closer to the truth on this one, too.

Because it was the nearest harbor with a harbor master, Twin Ports seemed the logical place to call. However, Abram knew a boat could be tied up most anywhere along the coast with little or no attention paid to it. This was a long shot at best. At his own desk, he dialed for information, and then called the number.

"Dean Orchard, harbormaster. Can I help you?"

Abram said, "I'm calling on behalf of Sheriff Larry Knight in Fairchance. I'm Deputy Abram Lincoln. We have reason to believe that a boat is somehow involved in a murder case we're investigating. It may or may not be registered, and we have no idea where it is. So I'm calling you first since Twin Ports could be where it's located."

"Any description of it?"

"No, I'm afraid not."

"Don't know if it's a fishing boat or a pleasure craft?"

"No. We have a key that appears to go with a boat. Someone here at the office said her father's pleasure boat uses a key like it."

"Ah. Well, we have been watching a cruiser that's not registered and is anchored in the bay. The only way we could tell if it's the right one would be to try the key. You want to bring it down here?"

"Yeah, I do. It's a bit rough today, though."

"You can say that again. I've heard that the Twilight Isle ferry was knocked out of service when the hurricane hit there. I guess some of the passengers got knocked around and some were taken to the clinic with broken bones. Anyway, the weather's supposed to be normal tomorrow, if you want to come down here then. I'll take you to the boat and we'll see if it's the one you're looking for."

"Ye…yeah. Okay. Thanks."

Before hanging up, he said, "Any names on those injured on the ferry?"

"No, just that some were hurt."

Abram hung up quickly, barely able to think. The ferry! Was there any chance that Astrid was on it? *If there's a problem, she's in the middle of it. I know it.*

He picked up the phone again and dialed the number for the house where she was staying.

A recording announced that the line was out of order.

No! How can I talk with her? Is she all right?

He would call Dean again.

"This is…"

"Dean," Abram interrupted. "Any chance you could get me out to Twilight Isle by boat tomorrow morning? My wife is there. I want to know if she's okay. Telephones are out."

"Let's see. Just a minute."

The pause had Abram on his feet, pacing as far as the phone cord allowed. The vivid memory of how frightened he was when he saw Astrid slashed by that crazy woman in the hospital. It was amazing that she healed so well. Of course, she was in the hospital because she stepped into a bear trap and could have remained there to freeze to death. He remembered also how close she had come to being shot, possibly killed, when she rummaged around that auto junk yard. Her misadventures had become legendary.

God, let her be safe, please.

"Yup. Okay, Abram. A friend of mine, Chris Lehman, will take you to the island. You plan to be there long? He needs to know if he should leave you or wait."

"Can't be sure, but if I find all is well with my wife, he can wait and I'll come back with him."

"Be here at 8?"

"I'll be there."

"Be sure to bring your key. We'll check that out, too."

*****

He was up at five Friday morning, anxious to be waiting for Dean before eight. Larry had given him the okay, even asked if he wanted someone to go with him. Why would he? It was agreed that he'd return today if he found that Astrid was okay. Of course she would be, but when his imagination started working there was nothing to do but get first-hand knowledge of the situation. After all, it was Astrid they were talking about. Astrid, the living magnet for trouble.

He turned on TV news. After pictures of damage from the tornado-like northeaster, the weatherman predicted a clear day with only occasional showers and much higher temperatures. The hailstones had melted fast, and most of the damage was from wind and lightning, though they showed some broken windshields hit by the icy stones.

Good. Abram left the house and headed for Twin Ports over roads cluttered with small limbs, water-filled potholes, silt, and paper. Nearing the port city, he had to swerve around a lawn chair in the road. Homeowners were outside studying damages. Houses had gutters and screens hanging by a thread. A huge old oak tree had split in half and smashed into a roof. Abram hoped no one was in that room when it crashed through.

"What a mess. It's worse than I thought. Seems worse the closer I get to the coast."

By the time he reached the harbormaster's quarters, it was nearly eight o'clock. He was greeted by a neatly shaved blond, six-four giant seaman.

"Abraham Lincoln?"

"It's Abram. No ham in it."

"Okay, Abram. I'm Chris. No tea in it." They laughed in unison. "Glad to meet you. You're coming back this morning, then."

"That's the plan if I find that my wife is okay. Telephone's out on the island. I tried again this morning. Still couldn't get through."

"Yup. That's the way it is all up and down the coast."

"I can't believe the damage the storm did over this way."

"Worse than inland, I guess."

Abram nodded.

"Is it calm enough to make the trip to the island, you think?"

"Shore. My Sadie can take some pretty rough water. But I didn't take her out yesterday. I'm no fool when it comes to a nor'easter like that."

They were talking just outside the harbormaster's small office. The door opened and an imposing man, dressed head-to-shoe in navy blue, emerged. Abram thought he needed a pipe in his mouth to complete the man-of-the-sea look.

"You're Abram, I take it. How about some hot coffee before you take off?"

"Sounds good to me. I didn't have coffee this morning, but if Chris is pressed for time…"

"Naw. Let's go in. Might as well get warmed up. It'll take about a half hour to get there."

Abram felt more relaxed than he did last night. Sleep wouldn't come as he thought of Astrid and what she might be going through on that island. Common sense rolled over him this morning telling him that if she were in trouble he'd have heard by then. He relied on that belief to keep him together while he took the time to have coffee.

"When you get there," Dean said while pouring the coffee, "might as well head in on the ferry side. The clinic isn't far from there. You'll find people around the ferry who'll help you out. They're close-knit on the island for good reason, I'd say, being practically isolated in winter. I love the sea, but you wouldn't catch me dead living on an island."

Abram and Chris laughed again. When he realized what he'd just said, Dean guffawed, too.

"I've become used to conveniences," he added. "Don't want to have to dig clams and trap lobsters to feed my family."

"Can't fault you there," Abram said. "It must take hardy people to do that."

Chris said, "Yeah, except for the summer complaints. They have it pretty nice. Live in luxury in city homes and enjoy summer days in island mansions. Nice work if you can get it."

They had finished their coffee before Dean said, "Hey, you want to check out that key before you go?"

"Sure do. Let's go."

In fact, Abram was anxious to see if he could fit another piece in the murder puzzle. A boat could answer some questions, but it also would open others. Where was the murdered woman planning to go, and why? How did Mayor Demetrie figure in all this? Were they involved in smuggling of some sort? Even finding a boat match to the key would not be the key to the most pressing question: why was Lisa killed?

CHAPTER 12

L istening to the wind beat against the house most of the night, Astrid found it difficult to sleep. Eddie had gone a bit crazy after hearing about the ferry accident yesterday. He would have walked out into that raging storm if the men hadn't held him back. Marvin had the best advice for action.

"Stay calm, Eddie. Corey has the short-wave radio. He'll find out details. Wait for him to come back."

Astrid was sure everyone was thinking, "He'll come back if he can stay on his feet in this wind."

While this house was probably the most beautiful one on the island, its situation atop a high cliff made it an open target for storms coming from any direction. Nothing on the shore was easily accessible from the hilltop. To reach the big boathouse where the descent was gradual it was necessary to go a half mile up the road.

When Corey returned, he did not have the news Eddie wanted to hear.

"All I could find out is that several people were taken to the clinic. No names yet. The ferry lurched suddenly in the wind and they were thrown against a rail. I don't know how serious injuries were, but the word is to stay put. Don't try to travel on the roads until the wind dies down. Roads are slippery and dangerous and pot holes are opening up. Tomorrow this will all be gone and it will be warm again. This was just a freak summer storm."

He looked around. In the candlelight, faces must have looked ghostly to him, given their anxiety. Astrid thought maybe he wanted an invitation to remain here rather than return to his quarters again in that driving rain. When nothing was said, he started for the door.

"I'd better get back to Millie. She's not afraid, but it sounds like the place is being torn apart. See you all in the morning."

Again, no one said anything, but they knew that it would be even harder to keep Eddie from barging out.

"We'd all be better off to stay together," Marvin said. "I suggest we each take a candle and head for the library. I'll get some snacks and water from the pantry. Remember, Eddie, it wouldn't make sense for you to get killed on one of the bad curves. I'm sure Aunt Helena will be just fine, if she's one of those hurt. If she isn't, she'll be put up at a nearby house. So let's not worry."

Today already looked better, with sun streaming through the bedroom windows. Astrid dressed in a hurry, worried that Eddie might have gone already to find Helena. She wouldn't be able to investigate the mysterious light now, but it would be okay. It was probably nothing more than her imagination working overtime in a normally quiet place. Then again, it was only Friday. The ferry must be running today. There might be time for the two of them to go snooping for answers about the light, if Helena didn't take off again to go the bank, presuming that she was not injured.

Chilled to the bone after washing up in cold water, Astrid dressed in her newest jeans for the warmth, as well as a sweatshirt over the only long-sleeve blouse she brought. She didn't anticipate being this cold when she packed her case. Absently, she flipped the light switch out of habit. As if by magic, all at once the light came on and a generator started up.

"Thank God. The power's back on. I wonder if the telephone is. Those linemen must have worked through the night. What a dangerous job they have. I don't envy them."

Brushing her hair, she recalled how long it used to be, so long that she had wrapped her silky blond braids around her head. Women in her family had always worn their hair braided. But she wanted a change and one day she decided to do it differently. She had it cut. When she walked into the hotel dining room that evening, everyone stopped talking and stared at her with her totally new look--short haircut and new dress. But the best was when Abram came in after working late. He couldn't believe his eyes.

What a sweet man. I do love him so.

She told herself not to get into that lonely mood again. She'd be home on Sunday. There might be word about Helena downstairs.

Everyone but Eddie had assembled in the kitchen. Astrid said good-morning and went to the side windows for a look at the morning-after damage. It was as she expected, flower beds sick, driveway littered with tree branches, small limbs strewn across the vast lawns. What a mess. Last night Eddie said he would get the gardeners in today to clean it up and plant new flowers.

Heading for the breakfast buffet, she said, "Everything's torn up out there."

Marvin agreed. "This was the worst I've seen in summer. Corey said that one window was broken by the hail—a garage window. I expected more than that would be broken."

Astrid took her breakfast to her usual chair at the table.

"Has Eddie gone already?" she asked.

"Yes." Marvin said. "He left ten minutes ago. We all decided to go, too. You want to come along?"

"Of course."

"Eddie went with Corey. We'll go to the clinic in my car."

"Clinic? Is Helena injured?"

"We don't know the extent of her injuries, but she's one of those sent to the clinic. I should have said that up front."

There'll be no hunting for that light now. We go home Sunday.

Disappointment slowly turned to self-criticism when she thought about poor Helena, injured and alone in the clinic. The light she looked at each night was nothing. At least that's what she kept telling herself. She felt childish for having had such a wild notion in the first place. There. That was settled.

"Sour grapes," she mumbled.

Sitting next to her, Dee said, "How's that? You want grapes?"

Astrid laughed and everyone stopped talking to find out what was funny.

"Oh nothing."

She waved her hand to the side, as if throwing the little joke away, but it wouldn't do. The others wanted more.

"I don't think there are any grapes here, Astrid," Jenny said.

"If they had a grape arbor," Charlie said, "it would have been ruined in the storm."

"You're right, dear," Jenny said. "I don't know if the local store has any, but I doubt it."

"What made you think of grapes, Astrid?" Dee said.

It was just too much. After all, she'd said it under her breath, not for everyone to hear. Why didn't they leave it alone?

Jumping out of her chair, Astrid stomped to the hallway door.

"For godsake, can't a person think out loud without being interrogated around here?"

She started for the stairway, feeling sheepish that she'd let herself get so disturbed by these well-meaning friends. After all, they were just teasing. It was Marvin who stopped her when he followed and called behind her.

"Astrid, no harm was meant. We're about ready to go to the clinic. Aren't you coming?"

Can't even have a good sulk. What made me fly off the handle like that? I must be stir crazy.

"Ya. I'm going, too."

She hoped her tone was more normal and not as silly as she now felt. Lately these odd emotional outbursts seemed uncontrollable.

"I know Helena will be glad to see you."

She followed him to the kitchen.

"Did we offend you, Astrid?" he asked.

"Not really. It was me being short tempered for no reason at all, I guess."

"We all understand. Confinement can shorten tempers. Even Dee snapped at me this morning. Nerves are on edge. We'll all start over."

She didn't know what was worse, her own outburst or this understanding, as if she were a naughty child but all was forgiven. Somehow, it had seemed like an intrusion on her thoughts, which she never intended to speak aloud. The fault lay with that stupid obsession she got over a little light shining at night, as if she were little Miss Marple, about to solve a mystery—only there most likely was nothing to it beyond someone's having left an upstairs light on.

Re-entering the kitchen, they found everyone standing and waiting. She told herself it was time to straighten up and act like an adult.

"I hope Helena isn't injured too badly," Jenny said.

Dear Jenny. Always concerned about others. Charlie should realize what a jewel he had for a wife. When he put his arm around her and steered her to the door, his unspoken appreciation surfaced.

"Let's get going and find out," he said.

Astrid's thoughts continued to drift back to the cases Larry and Abram now faced. How could they ever get answers when there appeared to be nothing to go on?

I wish I could get back to Fairchance and be with Abram, go to work on something meaningful.

It was rough riding over the littered road, even in Marvin's Cadillac. This lee side of the island had not been hit so hard as the northeast side, but pot holes and minor washouts were a challenge. No one talked, for which Astrid was grateful.

Located on the main street, the one-floor clinic gleamed white inside as well as out. Even the three nurses Astrid saw all wore white.

"Very clean place, anyway," she said on entering and quickly looking around.

A man, sitting near the waiting room door, looked up.

"What'd you expect? A dirty cabin? It's a medical facility, after all."

A closer look revealed, not an old man as she first thought on hearing his raspy voice, but a sandy-haired, deeply tanned man of 55 or 60, wearing a gray suit with black open-collar shirt. He must be one of the well-to-do on the island. Maybe a *real* resident. Astrid concluded he had to be wealthy to afford an obviously expensive suit and alligator shoes.

"Were you hurt on the ferry?" she asked, as if she cared.

"Naw. I cut my hand early this morning, when it was dark. I was getting a drink of water and dropped the glass on the floor. It shattered and I tried to pick up the pieces of glass. Cut my thumb kinda deep and thought I'd better get it dressed properly."

He held up his thumb, wrapped in a white handkerchief, now soaked red.

"Oh, so sorry. Can't you get in yet?"

The man looked her up and down.

"You're not an islander, are you?"

"No. I'm from Fairchance. You know it?"

An odd expression of surprise passed over his face, as if she'd just stomped on his foot.

"Yeah, I know it. What's your name?" he asked.

"Astrid. Astrid Lincoln."

Before she could ask his name, a teenager in white and pink candy stripe dress and white apron came toward them.

"I'll take you to Mrs. Reese now. Just follow me," she said.

She led the group to a small room where they found Helena sitting in a green chair. Eddie sat beside her, holding her right hand. She looked as pale as the sling that supported her left arm.

"You broke your arm?" Jenny asked.

"What gave you a clue?" Helena was seldom sarcastic, but obviously she was in pain. She quickly added, "Yes, I fell and broke my wrist."

"Why don't you tell them what happened?" Eddie said to Helena. "That is, if you're up to it. I'm sure everyone wants to know."

Astrid found a stool to sit on, while Charlie left to locate more chairs. He came back with folding chairs, like those used for an overflow of church goers on a Sunday morning.

After everyone was settled, Helena looked at Jenny.

"Sorry, Jen, I didn't mean to be rude just now."

"It's okay. You weren't rude."

"It was a rough day and night," Helena said. "When I started out, I didn't think it was much of a storm, nothing that would stop the ferry from its schedules. But by the time I got there, it had begun to blow very hard and hailstones pounded the windshield. I was afraid the stones would break the windows. Who knew it would get that bad? Did you ever see such a thing? Especially in summer like this. Anyway, I figured the ferry would have to wait once it got to the terminal."

"It hadn't arrived yet?" Astrid asked.

"No. It was just coming in. There are always some aboard who walk on and off, tourists especially who park on the mainland and ride over for a day. They go top side to the seats, and they disembark first. After the ferry docked, people began moving toward the ramp. Some were still coming downstairs. A powerful gust of wind slammed the boat. I could see it, and I thought it would tip over. It knocked people across the deck. I don't know how many, but one or two are hurt quite seriously, I understand. No doubt those who were on the stairs."

"If you weren't aboard, how did you break your wrist?" Dee said.

"Well, I could see that it was too rough for the ferry to go back across then, and rather than get into the line of cars waiting to go, I stopped near the ticket window with the intention of walking up to it and inquiring if they had any idea when it would leave next. That's when I was literally blown to the ground, my feet went out from under me and I put my arm down to break my fall. I broke my wrist instead."

"How awful," Jenny whispered.

"How did you get here?" Astrid said.

"I guess the telephones were still working, because the ticket seller got the two island ambulances out. They had me sit in front of one while they loaded what injured people they could into the back and brought us here. I don't know how they made it, the road had so quickly turned slippery. But they eventually picked up all who were injured, and this place got really busy. I had to wait hours before they could even X-ray my arm and then a lot longer before they put on the cast."

"She didn't get much sleep," Eddie added.

"No, they had to dig out some old cots for me and a couple others to sleep on. Not exactly like my own bed."

She looked into Eddie's eyes.

"I missed my bed," she said in a hoarse voice.

Astrid thought, *I know just what you mean.*

The severity of the storm was talked about for nearly 15 more minutes before a tall nurse with swan-like neck came in.

"There's someone here to see Astrid Lincoln," she said. "And you will all have to go out, too. We need this room for a very sick patient."

Astrid was the first out the door. She found Abram standing in the waiting room. Fighting tears that threatened to expose her misery, she ran to him and flung her arms around his shoulders.

"Abram! What are you doing here? How did you get here? Oh, how I've missed you."

He held her tightly and whispered in her ear, "I've missed you, too, Sweetheart."

When she pulled away, she said, "Shouldn't you be working?"

"I should be, but when I heard that some folks were injured on the ferry, I couldn't get in touch with anyone because telephones were out. So I contacted the harbormaster and he engaged a boat out of Twin Ports and the owner brought me here to find out if you were all right. I'm sure glad to see that you are."

"I am, but Helena isn't. She fell and broke her wrist."

"Oh. Sorry to hear that. How's she doing? Is it very bad?"

"She didn't get much sleep all night, but seems to be doing all right."

"You got it worse here than we did in Fairchance, but it was bad enough. I have a lot to tell you when we're alone."

The word alone was almost the tipping point for Astrid. A tear escaped, and she turned her head away not to give Abram alarm. But it was too late.

"What is it, Hon?" he asked. "You're not hurt, are you?"

"No, no, of course not. I'm just glad to see you, I guess."

"Are you ready to go home?"

How did he guess?

"I'm afraid I am. But I hate to go before the others do."

"How much longer were you supposed to stay?"

"Until Sunday."

"Surely everyone would understand if you go home with me. Talk with the host. Just tell him you're going home. A couple of days shouldn't matter to anyone."

He was right, of course, but she felt like a quitter.

"I'll talk with Helena first."

Helena was now on the other side of the waiting room. As Astrid moved in her direction, she heard Eddie ask, "Why can't I take you home now?"

"The nurse said I have to wait for the PA to discharge me. Getting out of these places is almost as hard as it is to get in to see a doctor."

When she saw Astrid at her side, she said, "What is it, Astrid?"

"I want to go back home with Abram, but I didn't want to leave without thanking you for your hospitality. I've had a very good time, as I know everyone has."

"But we didn't get to do our investigation, did we? I tell you what. Will you come back the week after next on Saturday and stay over until the last ferry on Sunday? We can go looking for the light, and see if we find something sinister."

"I think I was probably looking for something that just doesn't exist—a mystery of some sort. But I'll be glad to come back and visit again, if you really want to do that."

"I do. So it's settled. In two weeks. I'll give you a call. In the meantime, leave your things, rather than go back to the house now."

Astrid looked at Abram as he talked with Charlie by the door. She caught sight of that man she'd talked with and saw that he was going in to be properly bandaged.

"Helena, do you know that man just going into the emergency room?"

"Oh, yes. He's the son of Bella Beaumont, the woman our taxi driver told us about."

"Really? He looks so…"

"So sophisticated? If clothes make the man, then he's that alright. But believe me. I wouldn't trust him to change a quarter for me. He'd somehow end up with 50 cents. Just a bit on the tricky side, you know?"

"So his name is Beaumont."

"Actually it isn't. It's Donald Hollander. She was married and divorced twice. He's her only child. By her first marriage. When he was quite young, he left the island with his father, just recently returned, and somehow has money, but no one knows how he made it. Maybe his father inherited and passed it on to him."

"I see. Well, I'll be talking with you before two weeks are up. Give me a call, either at home or the office, Helena. Oh, you have a private telephone number. Would you mind if I have it? Otherwise, it's almost impossible to contact you."

Helena obliged with the number, and Astrid leaned over and kissed her cheek.

"It's been fun," she said as sincerely as she could muster.

CHAPTER 13

◆◆◆◆◆

Astrid was grateful that she didn't have to return over that bad road to pick up her clothing, but she would have to go shopping for a couple of items left behind. Just to be beside Abram, knowing she was homeward bound was enough to renew her spirit. They couldn't talk much over the noise of the boat's motor and crashing high waves, but after docking at Twin Ports and heading for home, they talked about their activities during the week. In her mind, Astrid had little to tell and encouraged Abram to do most of the talking. He explained, step by step, what had happened, that the kidnap case was still no closer to being solved, and that a body had been found.

"At first, I thought the body was Miriam."

Astrid said, "Oh…"

"But it wasn't her. Turned out to be a prostitute by the name of Lisa Smith. It was a terrible sight, Astrid. She was badly beaten. I hope I never have to see one like it again."

"I'm so sorry, Abram."

They rode in silence a mile or so before Abram went on with his report.

"I'm sure there is a link between the two," he said. "And somehow it seems that Mayor Demetrie is involved."

"Oh? How's that?"

"Well, the Rotary button for one thing. I found a Rotary lapel pin at the house where the body was, and Larry got the name of the man it belonged to because it was marked Secretary. It was the mayor's. And then there's the matter of the boat key."

"Boat key! What…?"

"I happened onto a key under some messy soap in the bathroom. When I took it back to the office, we were trying to figure out what it went to. Obviously it wasn't a door key or a lockbox key. While we discussed the possibilities, the new dispatcher came into the office, took a look at it, and said it was a boat key. She knew because her father has one like it for his boat. Then I called the harbormaster in Twin Ports to see if they had a boat in the harbor that hadn't been used for a while, and he said there was one and said for me to take the key to him so it could be checked out."

"So you did that?"

"Yup. I made arrangements for a boat ride to the island to check on you."

"To check on me."

"Well yes. I heard people were hurt on the ferry. I didn't know but what you might be one of them."

"I wasn't going anywhere on the ferry."

"Well you might have been for all I knew."

"Nonsense."

"So sorry for being concerned, my dear."

"You're aggravating at times," she said, invoking her favorite criticism of him.

"And just between the two of us, at times you can be a bit rash."

"Rash. Never heard such nonsense."

"Who's aggravating?"

Astrid had the feeling that he just trumped her, and gave it up.

"Well what about the key and the boat?" she asked, softening her tone.

"While I was at the port we all boarded the abandoned boat. Sure enough. The key fit. He wasn't sure whose boat it was, but on a long shot I asked him to call the mayor's house and inquire if he owns a pleasure yacht. Turns out he does, and he keeps it in Twin Ports. Mrs. Demetrie told us that."

"Well, there you are. Case solved. You're a regular Sherlock Holmes, Abram."

"Not quite. We can't arrest a person on circumstantial evidence. We need real proof that he is the killer. We know, because of the diary she kept, that he was one of her regulars, but beyond that we don't have any concrete proof of his involvement. These things we've turned up could mean his boat key was stolen by Lisa Smith for a quick get-away, the Rotary button could have been there for a long while, and on and on. If he is the guilty one, we have to have irrefutable evidence."

The Jeep crashed over a particularly deep pot hole. Rubbing her head after bumping the ceiling, Astrid said, "Maybe you should keep your eyes on the road instead of staring at me so much."

"The road isn't nearly as interesting as you are, my love."

"Ya, well, I'd like to keep my Jeep in running condition."

"Speaking of running condition…"

"Abram!"

His grin faded as quickly as his train of thought, and he said, "Of course, there is the code."

"Code? What code?"

"Her diary listed the names of her clients and the dates and amounts they paid for her services. The mayor was listed several times, but the usual information sharply changed after one date, and she began writing a code of some sort after his name. We don't yet know what it means, but we're guessing it's something to do with illicit business beyond prostitution."

"What is the code—numbers, letters, what?"

"Letters and numbers both. It's all so vague. I don't know if we'll ever figure it out. If we could, maybe we could tie it to the murder. It might even tell us who that is."

"And you say the code followed Mayor Demetrie's name."

"Right. The date and dollar amount for service stopped and codes were written, three times. And the letters weren't always the same. Larry wrote them down so we could study them more and try to make connections. It's worse than a jigsaw puzzle."

Astrid gave him a coy look of understanding--the infamous puzzle he worked on so long before finally proposing to her.

Thinking about what it could all mean, Astrid didn't hear what Abram said until he repeated it.

"Astrid? It's noontime, want to stop at Pascuale's Pasta and have a bite to eat before going back to work?"

"Good idea. I love his spaghetti sauce."

Pascuale's was a narrow building adjacent to the Fairchance Theater, with little more for atmosphere than a few Italian prints lining the walls and Italian music by Perry Como and Frank Sinatra playing softly. His food was an overnight sensation after he moved into town and set up the Mediterranean style eatery, a particular favorite of the noontime lunch crowd. As usual it was busy today.

On entering, they chose a two-seater, and, with orders placed, they leaned across the table to talk.

"What will you do today, Abram?"

"Most likely I'll keep beating the bushes to locate Nathan Demetrie. We went to his house yesterday and his wife said he wasn't home. We didn't believe her. She appeared devious."

"Yesterday! Then it must not have been as rough here as it was on the island."

"No. It was bad enough, and we got some hailstones, but as you see today it's all returning to normal."

"Maine weather!"

"I was glad I had the Jeep, though. I may have to buy one for myself."

"Your old truck could use an upgrade," Astrid said. "You've had the truck for years."

"It's a good old friend."

She leaned closer.

"Have the abductors said any more about Miriam?"

"Not a word, and they've been questioned day and night. I don't think they know where she is now."

"They left her there at that house where you found the body. Do you suppose the woman was murdered because she didn't want anything to do with kidnapping?"

"Could be. But Larry and I think there's more to it than just the kidnap."

"What else?"

"There's always the possibility of sex trade."

"Oh." Astrid was speechless for a moment. Then, "That's so horrible."

"It happens. They take a young person like Miriam and get good money for her to be trained as a prostitute."

"Slavery!"

"Exactly. What did you think human trafficking involved?"

"I don't know. I guess I didn't give very much thought to it, no more than maybe selling a person to work for a rich family, or something like that. No, I knew better, but it's not something we care to hear about."

"No. But I predict that we'll hear more and more about it in the years ahead."

"Maybe that's how the dead woman started, do you think? She was grabbed and forced into prostitution?"

"No, I doubt that," Abram said. "It's more likely she was in charge of her own game, with no pimp."

Meals came, and they concentrated on eating. Astrid felt like she had just been reprieved from a prison sentence. She looked over at Abram and smiled.

"What?" he asked.

"I'm just so glad to be back, talking with you, having a meal with you, thinking about a case together again. Nothing like it."

"Nothing?" He arched an eyebrow. "We'll see about that."

"You're a devil, Abram Lincoln." He faked a sulk. She added, "But I love you, anyway."

He abruptly changed the subject, just as he had done before.

"Now what are you going to do this afternoon? Going to *The Bugle*, I expect."

"Ya. I want to check with Beth and find out what, if anything, she has unearthed while we've been away. She's pretty ingenious, you know."

"So I've heard. Larry doesn't talk much about his home life, but once in a while he speaks of how brilliant she is. I guess the little boy is showing signs that he'll be the same."

He didn't notice that Astrid quickly lowered her eyes.

"Shall I keep the Jeep?" she asked.

"Of course. Someone will drive me home after work."

"Or I can pick you up if I stay at the office, and I probably will."

Already she could see that his mind had drifted to the case.

"Okay. Do that. And don't forget, this is all confidential."

CHAPTER 14

Astrid found Beth alone, busy at the computer. It was so good to be home, and the office really was her home away from home. She had spent less than a week on the island, but it felt more like a month. Perhaps she could enjoy a visit there sometime if Abram came along. If nothing else, it was a beautiful place.

Beth didn't look up when the door opened.

"That must be an exciting story," Astrid said.

"Astrid! Omigosh. What are you doing here?"

"That's a warm greeting, I must say. You want me to go back?"

"Lord no. I'm so glad to see you. But this is a surprise. You're not supposed to be here until Monday. Are the others here, too?"

"No. Abram got concerned when he couldn't contact me after the storm, so he hired someone with a boat at Twin Ports to take him over to the island. He heard about some people being injured on the ferry when it nearly tipped over. After he arrived we decided it was a good time for me to return with him. The others still plan to come back Sunday."

"We heard about the ferry. Well I am glad you're here. I'm ready to hand over the reins to someone else. But we've had some developments."

"In the kidnapping?"

"Uh-huh. But not just that."

A tingle of dread went up Astrid's spine. They couldn't know, could they?

"Griff got some confidential information two days ago. He's such a good reporter. Too bad he decided to take up police work instead of journalism."

"How did he come by this confidential information?" Astrid said.

"One of the rooky police officers overheard a conversation. You won't believe this."

"Try me."

"It seems that our mayor is not only involved with a prostitute right here in Fairchance, but that he killed her and…"

"Beth!" Astrid's voice made Beth jump. "Tell me you haven't spread that around. Have you told anyone else? Does Larry know about this?"

"No. Not yet. It will be a real scoop over all the other media. We thought we'd keep it under wraps until the paper comes out next week."

"Oh God, no. We can't do that. First of all there's no evidence that the mayor has done anything. And, beyond that, I'm not sure they have even said there's been a murder. You should have talked with Larry before giving credence to any of this."

"I don't understand. You've never hesitated to break a story, especially if it scooped everyone else, Astrid. What's different about this? Can't we just say it has been rumored…"

"No, we can't. We're not here to spread rumors. We work with facts, from the horse's mouth. And you know that. What's happened here? I hope it isn't Griff who's blinded you."

Beth stood up. She looked like she could kill.

"Well! I didn't know you were an almighty judge of others you never even met, or that you were suddenly the king of the hill here.

I thought whoever had the seat of editor-in-chief was the one who decided news content for the week. And I thought…"

She was cut off by Griff's abrupt appearance in the doorway.

"What's going on?" he asked.

"You must be Griff," Astrid said.

"Yeah. And who are you?"

"She's Astrid Lincoln, Griff." The angry tremor in Beth's voice remained.

"I see. Well, what's your problem?"

"She objects to the breaking news about the mayor. Says we can't publish it."

It was out of character for Beth to be defensive. Astrid knew she'd have to assert herself. She had no problem doing that.

"I'm the news editor," she said. "But if you prefer a more authoritative voice on the matter, I'll call Beth's husband, the sheriff, and we'll see if this is something he wants everyone to read when there is no certainty of its validity. Or have you already talked with him, Griff? I know you come highly qualified as a reporter, so I presume you didn't overlook obtaining confirmation of whatever information you heard."

He walked over to shake Astrid's hand, his eyes questioning, obviously disturbed by this confrontation.

"Glad to meet you, Astrid. No, I didn't confirm this news."

He gave Beth, whose face had turned a deeper red, the same inquiring look.

"Okay," she said. "It's my fault. I told Griff that I would talk this over with Larry. But I just didn't get the chance to do it. He's been running day and night trying to find the kidnappers. He's very frustrated. He hasn't said anything to me about the murder."

Astrid empathized with her friend. Like a dying person's life review, she saw a stream of mistakes she made over the past few years since coming to work at *The Bugle*.

"Don't worry, Beth," she said. "Like I said, there's no certainty there's been a murder. It's not too late to correct all this. It hasn't appeared on the street, so all we need do is go talk with Larry now."

To Griff she said, "Who gave you this information? Not that I mean to get that person in trouble, but whoever it was did speak out of turn."

Griff went to the sports desk and sighed heavily when he sat down.

"You know that sources are always confidential," he said.

"For the public and some officials, ya. But not for the newspaper editor. We must know to protect ourselves and protect the integrity of the newspaper. What if it's a bum off the street that came up to you and whispered in your ear that this is what he heard? We need a trustworthy source. I'm sure you know that."

"You're right, though I don't usually get news from bums off the street," Griff said. "Okay. I was talking with a new guy at the police station one day. I told him about some cases I'd covered in Hartford. Then he got all excited and told me about the mayor's rendezvous with a local prostitute. But he didn't stop there. He went on to say it appeared that the mayor had enough of the girl's services and murdered her. He went into details—enough so that I believed he told the truth. I asked him how he knew all this and he said he was hunting for a few pencils in an office one day when the sheriff and police chief stopped outside the open door in the hallway. He didn't want them to know that he was there, so he stayed quiet and listened. They exchanged this information. And they talked about where they had searched for the mayor, suggesting that he was missing."

Astrid could hear Abram's voice, "This is all confidential." How much could she say? She was right in the first place—talk with Larry. He'd pass judgment and admit, or not, about the murder.

She could see that Beth hadn't calmed down. She must be mortified to have been told she'd done something wrong, which she so seldom did. It was no pleasure for Astrid to cause her chagrin for trying to break a story that she was sure nobody else had. Worse yet, she must be thinking about how she might have had to face Larry, knowing he'd be upset with her for not going to him first. Abram would likely have some cutting things to say, too, if she should do that. Astrid knew the worst of it was that it would be just like her to pull the same blunder, given the opportunity.

"Okay," she said. "We all know it could have been much worse, and I'll tell you what. Let's just say that the information came to us anonymously, and we want Larry to confirm or deny it, and to offer his advice before doing anything with it. Sound okay to you two?"

"Of course. It's okay with me," Beth said.

"I'd say it's the only thing to do. And, the best part is that it's true, when you get right down to it," Griff said.

Ya, true. But oh how close it came to being a confession of guilt instead of a plea for direction from Larry.

Griff said, "I'll drive myself. You two probably want to ride together?"

"Ya," Astrid said. "I'll take Beth, and we'll meet you at the sheriff's office."

When he left the office, Beth said, "I'll bet you know all about this, Astrid. Did Abram tell you?"

This is all confidential.

"What Abram and I talk about is between the two of us."

Astrid reached for the phone on the first ring, thankful for the interruption. Before she could say anything, Larry said, "I want you to come to my office. If Griff is there, bring him, too."

"Okay, we're on the way."

If he was surprised to hear Astrid's voice, Larry said nothing, simply hung up.

"I guess your husband is calling a press conference, Beth. Let's go."

No other discussion followed, until they reached the steps of the sheriff's building.

"What's he going to say, Astrid?" Beth said in a sharp tone. "I bet you know."

"How the hell do I know what he'll say? Let's go in and find out."

This distrust from Beth hit a nerve, and she felt terrible about it since they were good friends. There didn't need to be friction if Beth had only done what she should have done in the first place, just talked with Larry. Suddenly she wondered, *What's going on? Aren't they getting along these days?*

CHAPTER 15

N ot quite ready to see her leave again, even just to go to her office, Abram watched until the Jeep left the court house parking lot and was out of sight. He had missed Astrid more than he'd ever let on. He never wanted to look weak in her eyes. A brick like her wouldn't understand this sentimentality of his. As far as he could remember, he'd been successful in hiding it.

For now, it was time to go to work. He bounded up the steps, nodded as he passed the white-haired man at the front desk, and hurried down to the locker room where he changed into uniform before going to Larry's office. All was quiet, though deputies hurried along the hall, whispering to each other as if sharing secrets. Larry's door was shut. He knocked and opened it. Finding Larry and Police Chief Patrick Rawleigh head-to-head in discussion, he was ready to leave.

"You're back, Abe," Larry said. "Good. Come in, take a seat. Just going over a few findings with Pat. We have a lot to discuss. I'm calling a press conference.

He looked at his watch.

"I expect reporters are already in the conference room."

"What's up?"

"We now know where Nathan Demetrie is. His body was found this morning."

"No! His body? He's dead? Where? How…?"

"Apparently he committed suicide. His wife found him hanging from a beam in their garage. She said he must have come home during the early morning hours. It was her habit to check all the doors to be sure nothing was open, including the garage, before she went to bed at about midnight."

"Did the coroner confirm a time of death?"

"They need to do an autopsy to be absolutely sure that he died by hanging and not from some other cause. He was vague about the time of death."

"Will you say that to the media?"

"We're not sure yet," Chief Rawleigh said. "We were just discussing how to break all of this to the public."

Larry looked more tired today than he did yesterday. Abram thought he must not be getting much sleep at all. Not surprising since he never gave up when he was on a case even when it meant spending most of the night here in his office.

"It's ticklish," the chief said. "There aren't many real answers yet. Like where had Demetrie been? Obviously he didn't want to be found."

"When I talked with Kay, she claimed she doesn't know anything about his activities. I think she's lying," Larry said. "But I'm guessing that suicide or not, the motive hinges on the Lisa Smith murder."

"And that's another question," Abram said. "Will you give out news of her death now? As far as I know word of the murder hasn't leaked yet."

Larry and Rawleigh exchanged questioning looks before Larry said, "Now is as good a time as any. We'll tell the truth, that we were waiting for the autopsy report before telling the media about her death."

"It shouldn't be questioned. It's only been a couple of days since the body was found."

Abram said that without thinking. Astrid, for one, would want to know why the delay anyway. But he didn't have to worry about that. She already knew.

One of the new deputies opened the door just wide enough to poke his head inside.

"Sir, we have two reporters and a photographer in the conference room. Should I tell them how long it will be before the conference?"

"Tell them it will be within fifteen minutes."

"Yes sir."

Abram remembered how shifty he had thought Kay Demetrie was when they questioned her. Just how much did she know about her husband? Could she have known that he was cheating on her? Might she have been jealous enough to kill him?

"Did you bring Mrs. Demetrie in for questioning?" he asked.

"Not yet, but we will. I talked with her after we got the call about her husband. I can see what you're thinking, Abe. Maybe she had enough of his philandering ways and decided to put an end to it. Who knows how far she might have gone to see that she wouldn't be shamed any more is anyone's guess. But for sure, she knows more than she told us."

Abram couldn't help but chuckle at that.

"Shamed by his philandering? What does her husband's death do for her?"

Checking his watch, Larry nodded.

"You've got a point. Not the greatest headline for her to endure, I'm sure. Maybe, in the long run, quiet cheating would have been easier to take."

Abram wanted to ask more questions but this wasn't the right time. He started to leave when Larry picked up the phone to make a call.

"Don't leave, Abe. I want to tell you something else. Pat, you go on in and offer the reporters coffee. Deputy Miles is there, I think. He can get the pot from the lounge. He already made fresh coffee."

Rawleigh left, and Larry spoke to the person who answered his phone call. Abram thought it was Beth because he mentioned Griff. After the call, Larry sat for a long while, apparently meditating, with his fingers steepled in front of his face.

At last, he said, "Abe, I'll come right to the point. We haven't had anyone fill the position of detective here since I left it to become sheriff. As you know two men have started out in that position. One left for a better post, and I had to fire the other one for taking advantage of a woman he arrested. Damned fool. We're still waiting for his trial to start. One thing I know is that I can trust you. You're a lot like me. You work hard and don't stop until you have answers. And you go home to your wife at night."

Abram felt his neck dampen in anticipation of what Larry was leading up to.

"Abe, I'm going to promote you to the position of Sheriff's Detective. I'll make that announcement public later, but I wanted you to know now. So what do you think? You up for it?"

"I'm...I'm overwhelmed. I'll certainly try. I hope I won't let you down."

"You work more like a detective than anyone I know, so you might as well have the rank."

"I'm speechless."

"You will spend more time investigating cases and you'll report directly to me, of course. I guess that won't be a great change.

I'll announce this promotion next week. We'll have some photos taken and be sure all the media have the news."

"All I can say is thank you."

"You deserve it. Now. Let's get this ordeal over with. I expect we'll be answering questions from now until the cows come home. You and I both know how reporters are. They seem to be deaf, but never at a loss for repeating the same questions over and over."

They both laughed. Each one was thinking that Astrid and Beth would not be amused.

On opening the door to the conference room Larry heard the first of the many questions he expected.

"Sheriff Knight," a voice screamed from across the room, "is it true that there's been a murder?"

The room was not full. Only a handful of reporters ever covered Fairchance news. Today three news outlets were represented, one as far as away as Waterville, one in Bangor, and *The Bugle*'s Astrid, Beth, and Griff.

Abram winked at Astrid as he followed Larry to the opposite side of the long table.

"If you will all hold your questions for now, I'd like to tell you why I have called this press conference. After I've finished, there will be 15 minutes for questions."

CHAPTER 16

A bram spoke Astrid's name once the conference ended, motioning for her to wait. She had hoped to talk with him privately to find out more about the latest shocker. She caught Beth's arm before she left the room.

"Beth, would you mind going back with Griff? Abram wants to talk with me for a minute."

"Sure thing. And Astrid, are we okay now?"

"Of course we are. Old friends like us stay friends even if they disagree now and then."

A quick hug and Beth ran to catch up with Griff, while Abram joined Astrid.

"I must say, Abram, Mayor Demetrie's death came as a surprise. What happened?"

"I shouldn't be talking about it, you know."

"Ya, I know. So what happened?"

She was as shocked as everyone else when Larry said the mayor was dead. The one thing he held back was how he died, but the sheriff insisted it could not be revealed until an autopsy was performed. Since all of the investigations were ongoing, he said, news was necessarily slow for the media, and he apologized for that. He promised to call another conference once they had more information to release. Astrid figured the next one would bring a great many more reporters. In fact, she could have warned Larry that his phone would be ringing endlessly as soon as today's conference was aired.

"Okay. When I got here, Larry told me the mayor was found by his wife this morning. He apparently hanged himself in the garage. She said he must have come home very late, and she didn't hear him. Larry's right that an autopsy needs to be performed before we'll know for sure that he wasn't murdered. At least, I think we will know then."

"Oh God, Abram. How many more are going to die? This is so incredible. You thought you were busy before. We'll be lucky if we see each other in time to say good morning now."

Abram reached for her hand.

"I won't let that happen real soon," he said.

"Suppose he did kill that woman and then hanged himself because he couldn't live with the guilt? Unless he left a note, we may never know. Was there a note?"

"I don't think so. We can't be sure about anything until an autopsy gives us answers. And we need to question everyone involved."

While he was talking, Abram appeared anxious to move beyond this latest tragedy. He turned his pencil over and over on the table and shifted his weight from side to side.

"Okay. What's up?" she asked.

"Who said something's up?"

So he was going to play the cat and mouse game. She recognized the scowl and squint while he talked about one thing and was dying to tell her something else.

"Look at you!" she said. "Just so smug. Tell me."

"Smug! Really?" He shrugged.

"Cut it out, Abram. Tell me."

"Let's see now. Maybe…no, it's not that. I guess I told you about the key and the boat." He shook his head. "I just can't think of anything else."

"Stop teasing. You've got something up your sleeve and I want to know what it is."

"If you put it that way. Maybe it's what Larry told me before the conference."

"What? What did he tell you? Come on."

"Oh it's not much, just that he's promoting me to detective."

Astrid, stunned for the moment, snatched up his hand and kissed it. But that wouldn't do for Abram. As he stood, he pulled her up with him and wrapped his arms around her for a long kiss.

"Seems like weeks since I could do that," he said, his breath catching with emotion.

"Detective!" Astrid managed to say once she could talk. "Abram, that's a big promotion. I'm so proud of you."

"Worth celebrating, I'd say."

Once again, he tightened his hold on her and kissed her hard. Her knees were giving way. She stiffened her arm against him and pushed.

"Now Abram, calm down. I don't relish the idea of sex on a table."

"It's looking more and more inviting to me."

"Forget it, you rutting buck. We've got work to do, and not funny work."

"You're a hard woman. Guess I'll just have to find myself a mistress."

She wrinkled her nose and poked a finger into his chest. "You just try it."

Abram pulled her to him again, but a commotion in the hallway outside the door drew their attention.

"Might as well see what's going on," he said, with a peck to her cheek.

He opened the door and fell backward when a heavy-set woman caved in against him.

"For godsake," she screamed, "you trying to kill me?"

"Didn't know you were standing against the door, ma'am. I was just coming out to see what was going on. Do you need help?"

She pointed to the tall, thin man across the hall.

"Ask that no-good husband of mine. Seems he needs more help than *I* can give him. Ask him where he spends his nights, comin' in at all hours. I'd like to know."

"She dragged me up here," the man said. "Sorry to bother you."

"Don't think that's all, mister." She pointed an accusing finger at him, while he slid farther along the wall. "You come in at nine this morning and think I ain't gonna get th' truth outa ya? Not this time, you don't get away with it. Officer, arrest my husband."

Abram scratched his head.

"Arrest him? On what charge?"

As fascinating as the tiff was, Astrid had to get back to the office. She nudged Abram.

"Gotta go to work," she whispered, and he nodded.

While she was making her way down the hallway toward the front door, Larry came out of his office and she heard him say, "What's going on, Abe?"

She left before she heard his answer, but was quite sure he didn't get a chance to answer before the woman did. Now how did that woman drag her husband to the sheriff's office? Astrid envisioned him trussed up in heavy ropes and her pulling him along by a rope slung over her shoulder.

She chuckled as she drove out the parking lot and headed back to *The Bugle* office. The poor man. Being married to her must be as pleasant as taking a slab of meat into a lion's cage for its first meal of the day.

Beth was on the phone when she walked into the office. Griff was gone. Astrid sat at her own desk across from Beth even though she knew Griff had been working at it. He could move to the sports desk when he returned. This was her place and he needed to understand that.

"Okay Charlie," Beth said, "that's all I have for now. Astrid just came in. You want to talk with her?"

Charlie. How did Beth reach him? The phones were out of order when she left the island. Astrid pressed number two on the phone dial.

"How's everything going, Charlie?" she asked.

"Okay here. We're all back at the house. Helena was released just after you left. I heard things are heating up in Fairchance. What do you know?"

"Well, I don't know what Beth told you, but Larry held a press conference and after he gave out word that a woman's body was found, he surprised everyone by saying that Mayor Demetrie died. So all that on top of the abduction of the teenager means there will be some late hours all around, I'd say."

"But Larry didn't say how the mayor died. Right?"

"That's right. They need to get an official cause of death from an autopsy before they'll release that information, he said."

"Beth says that new guy, Griff, has gone over to see if he can get something out of Mrs. Demetrie."

"Oh? I just came in so I didn't know that."

"She's a tough gal to interview. You remember when I tried to find out about her son. You'd think he was a Secret Service agent the way she avoided giving me direct answers. I can just imagine what her reaction will be to reporters asking about her husband's demise."

"Should be interesting to say the least. Are you guys okay over there? How's Helena feeling?"

"She went to her room when we all got back here. But I think she's okay, just tired after that long night."

"So we'll see all of you on Monday, then," Astrid said.

"Yup. I don't know about the rest, but I'm ready to go back now. It's been way too quiet since we got back here from the clinic. I guess you know what I mean."

"Let's just say Abram didn't have to do a lot of pleading to get me to come back with him. Glad I did. These cases are giving us more than we can handle."

"Fairchance will be reeling with rumors next week, you can be sure," he said. "Say, where's Will and Geena? Haven't seen hide or hair of them this week. I knew they were delayed but I thought they'd be here by now."

Should she tell him what she told Dee? She had only guessed at what Will was up to. Better not mention it.

"Gosh, I don't know, Charlie. I thought the same. It's a bit late now. Maybe they decided to take a different vacation. You know, just to get away from the rest of us."

"You're probably right. This wasn't a mandatory island visit. Sounds like you and Beth have things under control. If anything new develops…like a surprise autopsy report…give me a call."

"Ya, sure, except that you may not hear the telephone ring. Have a good time for the rest of the week. Oh, before you leave, will you tell Helena to call me here at the office tomorrow? I'd like to know how she's doing."

"Will do."

Beth worked for a few minutes on a sidebar for next week's newspaper before looking across at Astrid.

"You do know that today is my last day here, don't you Astrid?"

"No, I wasn't told."

"I want you to know that I've enjoyed this week, despite my poor judgment on the murder story."

Astrid held up a hand for her to stop.

"It's okay, Beth. I've done worse. We all have. You just had a temporary glitch in thinking. It's human. Besides, we caught it in time."

"I suppose so, but that's just it. I knew better. No excuses."

"Like I said, don't worry about it."

"I won't. I just wanted to tell you that I think I'm happiest being at home with my family. Even though this has been a good change for me, I now know after a week here that I don't want to be a career woman again. I had almost convinced myself that I wanted to go back to work, but I really don't. I hope you understand."

"I do understand, Beth. And to tell the truth I don't blame you. I think I'd like that, too. Maybe someday I'll take on that role with as much satisfaction as you have. It sounds pretty terrific. But I hope this little upset isn't the reason for your decision."

Beth shuffled papers on her desk before answering.

"It isn't, I assure you. I got pretty excited about the idea of breaking an important story, but in the back of my mind I knew about the second day here that this phase of my life was over. I want more family, and I want to be there for Larry when he needs me. I think we've both felt strain this week, strain that we didn't have before. I don't like that. To me, family must come first, and it's the way I want it."

"Then go for it. And, above all, be happy. Life's too short to work at something that eats away at you and tears you apart bit by bit with unnecessary stress. This *is a* stressful job. You're constantly under criticism—damned if you do and damned if you don't. No matter what you write, you're generally only fifty percent right. Believe me, the public is fickle."

Beth's hearty laugh was contagious. Astrid felt the warmth of their friendship once again. They had been friends too long to have a simple misjudgment come between them. She resumed typing, and Beth followed suit until the door opened. Astrid saw that Dee was as surprised as she was.

"Will," she said. "Where in the world have you been?"

"You're back, Astrid?" he said. "I thought you were all coming back Sunday."

"The others are coming back Sunday. I returned early. But why didn't you and Geena join the group?"

"I had to tend to some business."

Astrid felt sure she knew what that business was but wouldn't let him off the hook until he explained. If he had a new job, it meant another search for a sports editor. It was only fair that they know about it right now.

"Okay Will. Is it secret business?"

"Not at all. I went to Augusta to get information from a friend in the Child Welfare office."

"For the whole week?"

"No, Mother, not for the whole week. When I finished I took the family to Moosehead Lake to visit my brother and his wife. They have a cottage on the lake."

"Oh," Astrid said. She could have hugged him for not planning to leave.

"You through with the interrogation?" he asked.

"Your sarcasm is not appreciated, Will. I honestly thought you were going after a new job."

He looked shocked, then closed his eyes and laughed.

"A new job! I'm afraid I'd be in divorce court if I did that. Geena loves it here in Fairchance. So do the kids."

He rubbed his chin in thought.

"But if it weren't for them…"

"Ya, ya. Okay. What did you get out of that Augusta visit?"

"A few things. After I heard about that girl being kidnapped, I knew I had to do something more than just go on vacation. Geena understood. We have two daughters ourselves. I have a friend who has done a lot of research in human trafficking, though not many people know about it. It's seldom written about in this state, but it's a growing problem in the U.S. She gave me a bundle of information about what often happens to abducted children and women, as well as boys and men, and how they're lured or forced into labor or prostitution and other situations. I always thought the problem was more from country to country, but she said more and more incidents are being reported within our own borders. She had statistics of disappearances in Maine. It's a small percentage compared to more populated states, but because it's a profitable business, naturally it follows that ruthless flesh dealers are working their way here."

"How awful," Beth said.

"So do you have anything to help the authorities solve this case?" Astrid asked.

"Possibly. There's a human trafficking kingpin who has been working in Florida. They think he may have fled there when authorities began to crack down on his operations, and he may possibly be here in Maine. She—my friend—said they've been given that heads-up, but she doesn't know for sure if he's in these parts. Honestly, you can't imagine the fiendish people involved in this stuff. They get people of all ages, like I said, through force, coercion, deception. Those old enough are forced into slavery as laborers, or sexual services, bonded sweatshop labor, domestic servitude."

Astrid closed her eyes, seeing all the dreadful aspects of this trade. How could they possibly retrieve Miriam and return her to a normal life?

"Do you have the name of this so-called kingpin, Will" she said.

"He has used various aliases." He opened his notebook and read, "He's known by Tom Griffin, Alan Harrison, Don Hollander, and...."

"Hollander?" Astrid rubbed her forehead, thinking. "I heard that name just recently."

When it came to her, she reacted.

"I've got to go. If anyone wants me, I'll be at the sheriff's office."

"What is it?" Beth said. "You know something?"

"I sure do. Can't stop now. I'll tell you later."

Astrid heard Beth's words "What do you know, Astrid?" but continued out, ignoring the question. This was too important. She had to get to Abram and Larry. Could it be? Could it possibly be that she had talked with the man who kidnapped Miriam?

That question ran through her head over and over before she was at Abram's office door. Hollander. Why not? He looks slick enough to be a predator in any number of ways.

"Something wrong, Astrid?" Abram asked when she barged in without knocking. "You look like you're ready to take off for the moon."

"Maybe. I think so."

"Slow down, Hon. Sit down and tell me."

She couldn't sit down, needed to stay upright and pace, all the while trying to piece together the fragments she had in the kidnap case.

"Will was in Augusta this week instead of at the island with the rest of us. He got the name of the suspected leader of a human trafficking syndicate. Well, he didn't say it just like that, of course, but that's what I call it. And actually he got more than one name that he's known by. You'd think he'd be someone from New York, you know, where so many crimes are committed. But this criminal came out of Florida. Well, you remember Florida all right. It's a perfect gangster's haven with all the ports, and-so-forth. Huh! I wonder why they didn't name a place Gang Gables there. Huh! Well, they…the Augusta people…think that man is here in Maine, or he may be here in Maine. Why they know his name and haven't jailed him is more than I know. Well, maybe that isn't quite right. They don't know what name he's going by here, do they? They say they're keeping an eye on one person who may be the leader of this awful crime. Isn't that what they always say? Keeping an eye on someone? I wonder why that is. Maybe because they want local law enforcement to find out the truth instead of going after it themselves. Anyway, he's here. The criminal. He's here, Abram."

She finally looked at him and found that he was staring at her.

"Take a breath, Astrid. I think I followed that. You're saying Augusta knows the identity of the leader of a human trafficking gang, and that you know he's in Maine?"

"Ya. Exactly. He's not only in Maine, my love, he's on Twilight Isle, and I just know it. How do you like that? Huh? Huh? He's right under our noses."

She grabbed him by the shoulders and leaned in, face-to-face.

"We've got to get him, Abram. Can't let him slip away. Who knows, he may have Miriam. Let's get Larry and head over there."

"Astrid, just hold on a minute. You're going to bust a gut if you keep up like this."

He pulled her hands off his shoulders and she straightened.

"Will just came in this afternoon, did he?"

"Ya. Just now. He started to tell us about going to Augusta to see a friend who knows all about this stuff. When he said the name, I knew I had talked with him on the island."

She took a breath to say more, when Abram clamped his hand over her mouth to stop her.

"You keep saying you've talked with him. Who the hell is he?"

"I told you. It's Don Hollander."

"You didn't tell me, but now that we have that much, would it be too much if you told me where you met the guy?"

"I was sure I had told you. Are you sure of that? Well, it doesn't matter. I think you may have seen him, too. At the clinic. He had cut his hand and was there to get it treated. A well-dressed man, maybe in his fifties. He sat with his hand held up like this all the time he waited."

She crooked her arm and held her hand upward.

"I think I do remember him," Abram said. "Had light hair and a dark tan."

"Ya, that's him. Probably got that tan in Florida. You know, golfing and fishing, lounging by the pool. He looked like that kind of guy to me. The real dapper, showy kind. I'll bet he had plenty of arsenal on him, too. A gun, a knife…"

"You don't think if he snaps his fingers a regiment will ride out to his rescue, or maybe a masked man will show up yelling, 'Hi, ho Silver. Away.'?"

"Abram!"

"You really should write westerns, old gal. I've seen you half-cocked before, but I think this may be just a bit overboard. But we can take what you think to Larry."

She looked at her watch.

"Oh damn. The last ferry coming to the mainland is at 4:30. We won't have time to get there and back"

She thought for a minute as they walked toward Larry's door. Then she stopped.

"I know. We can go by boat. We did it before."

"Don't leave the dock just yet, Astrid dear. Larry will tell you why."

"I can't see any problem. He's wanted anyway. Just pick him up and lock him up. Even if he isn't our man, you can turn him over to whoever wants him."

"It's just not that simple. Like I said…"

"Some kind of secret?" she interrupted.

"What a devious mind. No, just plain common sense. We do have to practice it in this business of maintaining law and order, you see. We follow rules."

"I get it. You're saying I don't use common sense."

"Why, I would never say that. I value my teeth too much."

"You're still an aggravating man, Abram."

CHAPTER 17

As they bantered in the hallway, the door swung open, and Larry rushed out, obviously on the move, shoving between them. They jumped out of his way.

"Come on, Abe. Hi Astrid. We need to go see Mrs. Demetrie right now. I'll explain on the way."

Astrid started to follow them down the hallway.

"Not you, Astrid. Sorry. This can't be released just yet. Abe can tell you more tonight."

She clenched her teeth nearly as tight as she fisted her hands while she watched them go through the front doors. Something big was happening and she wanted to know what. It wasn't fair. After all, Abram had told her all about the cases until now. For that matter, why didn't Larry confide in Beth?

Why can't I follow through? I don't have to report it if he wants to keep it quiet. They're spinning their wheels and I can take them to a real criminal. It's not fair. What's so important about Mrs. Demetrie? Damn.

While she rolled questions over in her mind, she stared down at her dirty white sneakers, ignoring the fact that she was in the center of the hallway until a burly man with a four-day growth of whiskers and an odor to put a skunk out of competition nearly knocked her down.

"Get out of the way, bitch. Other people walk here, too."

"Hope you enjoyed accommodations here. Better go home and get acquainted with soap and water."

"Bitch." His growl echoed down the marble walls.

One of the great unwashed. You'd better hurry out before I pull down that fire hose and blast you out. I wonder why some men let themselves get so filthy that you could smell them across a tennis court.

She slowly walked to the front entry, all the while considering what she could do on her own. While the officers were concentrating on Demetrie's probable suicide, she remained certain that she could bring in the boss of a gang of human traffickers and maybe, just maybe, she could find Miriam Neal. Could she do it without Abram and Larry? Don Hollander was a virtual prisoner himself on that island. He was likely hurting from that cut and taking it easy at home, wherever that was. She could find out easily enough. Just ask Helena.

Now, sitting in her Jeep, trying to decide how best to get there and what to do then, she asked herself if it would be wise to tackle this on her own. The men who were still there at Helena's house could give her a hand if necessary. What about island Security? That office should help. Oh, undoubtedly they would need some legal papers, a warrant anyway. Security could get that. What about the right of citizen's arrest? If this didn't qualify, then what would? Why would Larry object to doing that? Well, it must be done. Better to ask forgiveness after the fact than to ask permission beforehand.

That's it. I can take the ferry in the morning. Helena and Eddie are home now. They can direct me to the Security office. From there it will be easy. Just go to Hollander's house and arrest him. He'll be so surprised he won't know what hit him. Larry can take the credit afterward, even if he does blow his stack. This is the time for action. I don't know what he's doing about Demetrie's suicide, but I'm a whole lot more interested in saving a girl's life than hashing over who was where when a man killed himself. The man's dead. Let's save the living.

Slamming her foot on the accelerator, she felt the wheels spin beneath her when she sped out of the lot.

"A bit of rubber graffiti for your parking lot, Larry," she said. A feeling of deviltry exploded into a loud laugh. *"Just you wait, Mr. `iggins, just you wait and see,"* and she laughed again. She always did empathize with Eliza Doolittle.

*****

Abram waited for Larry to tell him about this emergency run to Demetrie's home. He would like to have pursued the line that Astrid presented and try to bring Miriam home from her abductors, if indeed that Hollander guy was the guilty man. But it was no use trying to stop Sheriff Larry Knight once he set his sights on whatever chase he began. Right now it appeared that Demetrie was the priority in his book. Probably correct, too. He usually was right in his hunches and deductions. Which was it this time—a hunch or had he actually figured out something important?

"You have something new, Larry?"

"Huh? Oh." His distraction signaled introspection not unlike when he worked on a recent case that he solved by concentrating on all the local clues and tying them together. True, it wasn't as explosive as this case involving the city's mayor, but it deserved considerable media attention since a statewide gambling racket was shut down because of his attention to detail right here in Fairchance.

"Yeah, I'm thinking that we've made a wrong assumption concerning Nathan's death," Larry said. "I'm almost certain it was murder. He was killed somewhere else, taken to the garage, and strung up in order to make it look like suicide."

"That's a leap. What makes you think that?"

"The time of death, for one thing, and the cause for another. The medical examiner and I just talked. He said Demetrie had been dead a couple of days before he was found. You recall that Mrs. Demetrie said he must have come in long after she went to bed, when in fact he was already dead and she knew it."

"How did the coroner say he died?"

"He thinks it was poison. But a full autopsy needs to be completed."

Abram thought about that before saying, "It would take a pretty strong person to lift his dead weight. His live weight must have been at least one-ninety."

"It would take at least a couple of strong people, I'd say. I don't know. I just think there was some sort of conspiracy in this, right from the beginning with the murder of Lisa Smith and now Nathan Demetrie."

"But what about the girl—Miriam. You think any of this is linked to her?"

"I wish I knew. Could be, I suppose. The fact that the Wards directed us to that house might suggest a connection. But what? We haven't been able to come up with anything to connect the kidnapping to the killing. Not yet anyway. If Miriam was taken by a sex trafficking gang, it's possible the prostitute was involved, I suppose. From the diary, we know that the mayor had relations with the Smith woman. What we need is solid evidence of the tie-in. The answer is probably in the code Lisa Smith used in her little book. I haven't come up with a solution to all that. Not yet."

They were at the Demetrie residence. Before they got out of the car, Abram asked another question.

"You don't think Mrs. Demetrie had anything to do with her husband's death, do you?"

"I wish I knew, Abe. It would make our job a lot easier. As it is, we'll talk with her again and see what we'll see."

The maid answered the doorbell this time. She looked frazzled, her short hair sprouting around a traditional servant's cap. Abram found that cap and the skimpy white ruffled apron over black dress pretentious, just like the whole house and the people in it, especially like Mrs. Demetrie who greeted them with all the charm of a queen walking into the elegant foyer. Her navy blue suit, white gloves, hat and veil were right out of the forties.

"My dear Larry. As delighted as I am to see you again, I cannot stay long. I am on my way to the funeral director's office to discuss services and burial for my husband and my son."

"I understand, Kay. I'll try not to inconvenience you more than necessary. I want you to come to the station so that we may go over more details concerning your husband's death."

"Right now? But I have made this appointment. Mr. Thompson is expecting me. Really, Larry. I must do this."

"Pick up that phone over there, call him, and tell him you will be delayed for maybe an hour."

His firm tone left no doubt that she would go with the sheriff and not directly to the funeral home.

"Well!" she said, switching around and raising her chin. Nevertheless, she walked to the phone and dialed, all the while mumbling about how inconvenient all this was. "If Nathan were here, he wouldn't put up with this insolence."

They did not cuff her, but as soon as she finished the phone conversation, Larry and Abram each took an arm and walked her to the sheriff's car for a ride in the back seat. They repeated the manner of walking her along and into the sheriff's offices, down the hallway to an interrogation room.

"Would you like coffee, Kay?" Larry asked after she was seated at the table and had turned back her veil.

"No. I would not. What I'd like is an end to this nonsense. What is it you want from me? I called you this morning with what I remembered about my daughter. She arrived home very late and was noisy enough to wake me up. Most likely drunk. That was about two o'clock. I went downstairs to see what was going on. She was leaning over the kitchen sink, throwing up. I don't know anything else. When I got up this morning, I planned to use the car. That's when I found Nathan. I just thought you might want to know that information in case Tracey could shed light on Nathan's actions. Maybe she talked with him. I don't know."

She did the little handkerchief thing again, tapping along each eye, as if she had shed one tear from each.

"You said you didn't see or talk with Nathan all evening," Larry said while standing with his back to her.

"That's right."

"And everyone else in the house said the same. You told me that they all had said they didn't see him."

"That's right."

Larry quickly turned and leaned over the table to look her straight in the eye.

"Yet now you say your daughter came in at two o'clock?"

"Well, yes. When I remembered that, I called this morning to let you know. I thought…"

"Just what did you think, Kay? That you could suggest that your daughter may have known more than she told us? That by her late-hour arrival home she might have had some part in killing her father?"

She clamped her lips together, leaving only a line of mouth. Abram thought she would not say more. But he was wrong.

"Killing him! He committed suicide. Why would you say such a thing?"

"Because he did not take his own life. He was murdered."

She appeared genuinely stunned.

"No, that can't be. There wasn't any blood around. He hung himself."

"No blood, that's right enough. But his death was homicide."

"If you think that, then what happened? You have that all figured out, do you?"

"There's more than one way to end a person's life. For instance, garroting or choking with the bare hands. Poisons will also do it. But you probably know more about all of that than I do, since you've studied methods of each."

Her eyes widened.

"What in the world are you talking about? I haven't studied any such thing. I know nothing about poisons."

"Your daughter has a different story. In fact, she should be here by now. I had a deputy pick her up. Just a minute while I get her."

"Why get her? She'll only lie."

"We'll see."

Larry left the door open while he went down the hall. He returned, guiding Tracey by the arm.

"Right in here, Tracey. Sit here, beside your mother, please."

Larry and Abram sat across from the two, and Larry resumed his conversation as if they'd not been interrupted.

"You see, when Tracey called me this morning she said you went to the library weeks ago, and took out a big book on poisons, as well as a collection of Agatha Christie stories. As we all know, she was an authority on poisons and often used them in her murder mysteries."

"Why did you say that, Tracey?"

Tracey focused on Larry, with her head held high, apparently up for the challenge.

"I said it because it's true."

"I'm inclined to believe her," Larry said. "In fact, I checked the library and was told that you did, indeed, check out these books."

He leaned his chair back in a relaxed position, and folded his hands over his belly. Abram felt like a useless third wheel, dumbfounded by Larry's having dug up this information.

"You can't take the word of a drunken teenager. She doesn't know what she's talking about."

"Maybe not," Larry said. "But what she told me was that you brought the books home, laid them on the hallway table before taking them up to your room. You went off somewhere in the house before she came in that day, and she stopped to look at what the books were. She said she thought it an odd collection, especially since you usually read only cheap romance novels."

"You're crazy," she said to Tracey. "If you saw such books, they certainly weren't mine."

"Whose then?" Larry asked.

"It's just her word against mine. Why do you believe her? The only books she opens are school books. And that's seldom enough, at that."

She wiped her neck with the lacy handkerchief.

"Let's get down to what she says about coming in so late. By-the-way, how old is your daughter?"

"Why, she's fifteen."

"Fifteen. And out drinking all hours of the night."

"What can I do? She does nothing that I tell her. If I tell her not to go out, she goes anyway. Defies me. Nathan is the only one who can…or could control her."

Tracey giggled.

"Guess I can have some freedom now, Kay."

"You call your mother Kay?" Larry said.

"Sure. That's her name."

"You see what I mean, Larry? She's insolent."

"Tracey, you came home at what time?"

"Two o'clock."

"And your father's body was hanging in the garage?"

"Yes."

"You didn't see it when you went out for the evening?"

"No. I was picked up by my boyfriend. I didn't go through the garage."

"But you came in that way?"

"Yes. I always do. It's the quietest way to get in."

Again Tracey giggled.

"I'm warning you, Larry Knight," Kay said in a hushed, unsteady voice, "That is all a lie. I'm not without influence in Augusta. I'll see to it that you lose your position if you take that girl's word over mine. I'll publicly denounce you."

With a trembling hand, she brushed an edge of the veil from her face.

"Calm down, Kay. When we talked with you yesterday, you were in high heel shoes. Did you just come in or were you just going out?"

"I was planning to go out when the storm cleared."

"And how were you planning to go?"

"I was going to drive myself, of course."

"Did you do that?"

She paused for a long time before she said, "Yes, I did."

"Interesting. You just brushed the body aside and backed the car out, is that right?"

"I...there was no body there then."

"Of course there was. Nathan had been dead twenty-four hours when we talked with you."

"You lie."

"No, Kay," Tracey said. "You lie. You did kill him."

"This is disgusting," she said. "Tracey will say anything against me. For some reason she hates me and she's told me so many times. I don't know what's the matter with her. She just wants to run around with every bum that looks at her with a twinkle in his eye. Nathan took a firm hand with her. He would ground her for a week at a time, but it never did any good. How could it? He wasn't home enough himself to know whether she was there or not."

Her voice had become stronger and angrier. Abram watched and listened with the hypnotic wonder of a boy watching his first strip tease act.

"Who is Everett Gibson?" Larry asked.

If he had held a gun to her head, Kay wouldn't have looked more stunned and sick. Her color turned red and faded to gray. Abram was ready to rush her to the ladies' room in case she was sick.

"Who?" she asked.

"Everett Gibson. You do know him, don't you, Kay?"

Tracey turned to look at her mother.

"I guess you're caught, Kay," she said with a snort.

"That's a low blow, Larry. How did you...? Oh, of course. Tracey."

"He's a strong man," Larry said. "Did he help you with your husband's body?"

"No. No. No." She slapped the table with each denial. "We may have wanted him dead, but we did not do it. I'm telling you the truth. Nathan had his forays to houses of ill repute, and I knew that for years. But I wouldn't kill him for that. He didn't care what I did, as long as I put up with his womanizing and we both were discreet. I haven't seen Everett for two weeks. He has a good bank position. You don't have anything on him, no reason to involve him in all this."

How interesting, Abram thought, *Nathan and Kay were both loose as a goose. Where will Larry go from here?"*

"Then who did help you? It had to be either a very strong man, or even two strong men to lift the body up."

"He didn't deserve to live," Tracey blurted. "Kay may have killed him, but he got just what he deserved."

Abram nearly fell off his chair. *Now she's helping her mother? Or is she? It's a tangled mess.*

"Why did he deserve to die?"

"He just did."

"Why do you say that, Tracey? Did he hurt you?"

"He…he was mean. Real mean."

"Do you share that judgment, Kay?"

"He was more severe than I was," she said. "But the kids both needed a strong hand."

"Nice, Kay," Tracey said. "I defend you and you blame me, like always."

"Well, tell me Tracey," Larry said, "what do you mean when you say your dad was mean?"

"He just was. Once he hit me so hard I had a black eye."

"Kay? Is that right? Did your husband hit the children? Did he hit you?"

She turned her head away from his demanding eyes. It appeared she wouldn't answer the question, but Larry waited. When she looked back at him, she became arrogant again.

"He did. He couldn't control his temper. When I heard about that Smith girl's death, I knew he had done it. By then it was too late."

"Too late? For what?"

She studied her hands without answering.

"What was it too late for, Kay?"

"By the time I saw on the news that she had been brutally killed, Nathan was already dead."

That silenced everyone. Abram thought, *Ask the question, Larry. Did she kill him?*

And then Larry did ask, "Kay, did you kill Nathan?"

"Yes. I killed him. When I found out what that cheap woman was and that he saw her every week, that he made love to her at that shack, I couldn't stand the humiliation any longer. I poisoned him, and got help in hoisting him up to make it look like suicide."

"Who helped you?"

Kay looked at Abram and then at Tracey.

"Well? You want to tell him or shall I?"

Now Tracey began to cry. All her haughty manner melted like the evil witch in the *Wizard of Oz*. She stood up as if she were about to run.

"Sit down, Tracey," Larry said. "Answer the question. Did you have a hand in this?"

"Oh. Alright. Yes, but she made me do it."

"Who made you do it?"

Tracey pointed at her mother.

"Kay." Sobbing uncontrollably, she continued, "She said she'd kill me, too, if I didn't help her with his body. It was awful. I didn't want to do it, but she made me."

CHAPTER 18

$\cdots \blacklozenge \blacklozenge \blacklozenge \blacklozenge \cdots$

Abram had a lot to tell Astrid when they were alone in the evening, sitting together on the sofa. After he related the shocking confession that Kay and Tracey made, Astrid thought she should tell him about her plan for tomorrow, but just when she was going to do that, he had more to say.

"You know, those two, Kay and Tracey, are two of the coldest people I ever ran into, especially for women. First the mother turned in her daughter, and then the daughter pointed the finger at her mother. They're both self-indulgent, but I must admit I felt sorry for Tracey. She had a brutal father and a self-absorbed mother. I don't know what will become of her."

"Children generally grow up reading their parents very well. They learn to roll over them. But when she was threatened by her own mother, I guess Tracey didn't have much of a choice. I suppose she could have contacted the law, but kids that age tend to fear the law, I think."

"Did you study child psychology?" Abram asked.

"No. I just grew up not being able to communicate with my parents. And I understood both of them. If it hadn't been for my grandfather, I might have treated my mother as badly as Tracey treats hers. My mother thought all girls should be little angels, which I just couldn't be. And my father was an unreasonable man. He was a bully and a control freak. I resented both of them for what I interpreted as underrating me, possibly hating me. Like I said, my grandfather was a good influence. He was my guiding light, especially through the tough teen years. He helped me gain self-confidence."

"I had no idea. You know, we really should talk more about ourselves. I didn't tell you about my sister, and now you reveal this about your childhood."

"I suppose you're right."

Can there be a better time than this to ask.

"Abram, do you think you'd like to have children?"

She was prepared for him to answer that he didn't want any.

"Where did that come from? Of course I would. Why do you ask?"

"Well, that's something else we haven't discussed. With the kidnapping and with this out-of-control teen becoming an accomplice to murder, though that's more the fault of the parents, of course, I just thought maybe you would want to keep our life the way it is, just the two of us, without complications of children."

"I love children. They don't have to become abnormal, you know. I'm sure we'd be good parents, listen to them, set rules. Well, just all the things that kids need."

What a relief she thought.

*****

No one but Helena knew that Astrid would be back on the island today. In another day *The Bugle* group would all return to Fairchance, but it didn't matter to her. She had too much desire to find out about that light and see if someone was hidden in Mort's house to wait any longer. After calling Helena late Friday night and telling her she'd be there early, she said nothing to Abram until they were up and having coffee. It was very early since Abram had to work.

"Nice to see the sun shining. Looks like it'll be a hot day," he said.

She looked over her coffee cup at him.

"Honey, I think I'll go to the island today and pick up the things I left."

"Really? But you just got home yesterday."

"I know, but what I forgot was a notepad with important notes on a story I'm writing this week. I really need to get it."

His raised eyebrow said he was suspicious of her motive, but much to her relief he didn't say the obvious, that one of the others could bring it to her tomorrow.

"Okay. Whatever you're really up to better not involve something that the law should handle."

"Trust me, it won't."

Trust me? How it just tripped off her tongue as if she meant it.

"When will you be back?"

"Around suppertime, I think."

"Okay. I have a busy day ahead of me, so I'd better head for the office. You be very careful, Astrid, my love. Promise?"

"I promise. Don't worry."

With a kiss, they parted.

That was two hours ago. Now she was on the first ferry crossing to the island, leaning on the high rail to watch terns in close formation skim over the calm water. She had read that there were more than 3,000 islands off the coast of Maine, an incredible number, she thought. Maine offered so much: Salt water and islands, acres and acres of wild blueberries, fir and pine trees, pink granite of Acadia National Park downeast, Mount Katahdin up north, farms like her family's, rivers and lakes. It was, indeed, a beautiful and grand state. No wonder so many came to spend summers. No wonder native Mainers were jealous of what those "from away" folks had, and not always receptive to the city manners and accents. Mostly retirees settled in waterfront mansions, like Helena's, even infiltrated inland towns and cities where manufacturing had disappeared as CEOs found cheaper labor offshore in poor Third World countries. Out-of-work employees moved, too, in search of new jobs and sold homes on the cheap, only to learn after the influx of the wealthy, that those run-down houses had been bought and upgraded, creating astronomical assessments that led to sky-high market values.

Nevertheless, Astrid contemplated her good fortune to have been born and reared in the Pine Tree State. She also thought how people treated it callously. The thought intruded when she smelled the acrid odor of cigarette smoke. Passengers had left their automobiles to come upstairs and enjoy fresh morning air while polluting it with smoke. It was a disgusting practice to one with a keen olfactory sense.

A three or four-year-old boy ran over to her, smiled, and said, "Hi." He was irresistible. Astrid wanted to pick him up, but knew that his parents weren't far from him and would be alarmed if she did that. Seeing him, with his soft curly blond hair and rosy cheeks, reminded her of the talk she and Abram had last evening. She should have guessed that he would like children of his own. And what a good and loving parent he would be.

"Well, well, Miss Astrid Lincoln of Fairchance. What brings you to our fair island again?"

She recognized his voice before looking around. Rats. What were the odds that they'd meet like this?

"It's *Mrs.* Lincoln, Mr. Hollander."

"How about that? You found out my name. There must be some attraction for you to go to that trouble. Never mind answering.

I know you'd deny it even if you were burning to become better acquainted. I know I am."

You low-life scumbag. I want to see you behind bars, that's what I want.

She refused to engage in a conversation with sexual overtones. "I am spending the day on the island with my *friends*."

"The Reeses?"

"Ya."

She had emphasized the word friends to tell him he was no friend of hers. He sidled up beside her at the rail, and she could see that the cut hand was now amply bandaged. Ordinarily she'd inquire of a normal person how the hand was doing. But not Don Hollander. She'd be happy if his hand dropped off into the bay water.

"That's great," he said. "Why not stop on the way to the Reese cottage and have morning coffee with me?"

Out of the corner of her eye she saw him leaning toward her. When she didn't reply, he hastily added, "My mother is always happy to have a guest. And she makes the best doughnuts of anyone around these parts."

What a con artist. Wonder if this is one way he picks up unsuspecting women to sell into service elsewhere.

Despite her reservation about being alone with him, she began to think that with his mother there she'd be safe. And once she learned more about him, maybe where outside doors were located in the house, then she'd know how to direct authorities to deliver the warrant for his arrest. If she could find out more about his coming and going, they'd know what time of day to do it.

"Lot of seagulls out there this morning," he said, as if he'd just casually stepped beside her and said hi.

She grinned, hoping to accomplish a Joan Fontaine-like smirk.

"They're terns." Why she said that, she didn't know, except that it somehow seemed right to correct the big-time gangster.

"Terns? Not gulls?"

He was laughing at her. She could see it in those colorless eyes. Baiting her on. Still she continued as if unaware of his cuteness.

"Ya. They're smaller than seagulls and some of them have black heads. That's how you can distinguish them."

"Well, you seem acquainted with saltwater life for a landlubber. Did you live by the ocean in your lifetime?"

And you seem ignorant about saltwater life given that you lived here. Pulling my leg, are you?

"No. I was brought up on a farm. Inland," she said.

She'd learned about gulls and terns from Helena, but he didn't need to know that.

"Have you always lived on the island?" she asked.

"I was born here, moved away to less rustic areas for about 20 years to earn my fortune, you might say. Nothing like being independently wealthy."

Don't be so smug. Others, like me for instance, are also wealthy, and don't go around boasting about it.

"Do you have your own family?"

"If you're asking whether I'm married, no, I'm not. And I've got no kids. That makes me not just eligible, but a great catch for some lucky girl. My mother's the only family I've got. I came back to help her. She's getting old, lives alone. I don't plan to stay here, though. You know how it is. You can't go home again."

His laugh, like his manner of talking, was arrogant. Astrid looked directly at him and saw the face that matched the sound-- dimpled cheek, eyes the unusual color of clamshells, arched brows, wavy light hair neatly trimmed and unruffled by the sea breeze. He was the epitome of self-centered. He stared at the island ahead of them. His expression of disdain disturbed her. It seemed to show a grim promise of danger. Obviously he carried inner anger, like that of a spoiled child, ready to cause as much trouble as possible. He carried it in his better-than-everyone body language and askance gaze as he spoke to a person.

"I'll get away real quick-like when Ma cashes in." Hunching his shoulders, "Who knows?" he said in whisper-quiet introspection and turned his attention to Astrid. She almost shuddered at his sudden change and this concentrated focus on her.

"Maybe I'll head over Fairchance way real soon. I can see from here that there are very tempting treats there. Who knows?"

He was assessing her like a horse trader assesses a young filly, making that smooth m-m-m sound as if he liked what he saw and was about to lay down cash for her. Everything in her said not to let him get too close. Stay away. Don't step into his web of deceit. Go directly to Helena's.

You've been through this kind of trap before. You know what he is.

Not too long ago she wouldn't have thought twice about going with him, even doing battle with him, if necessary. She used to believe she could defend herself against just about anyone, man or woman. But now after being unsuccessful at self-defense, she knew that one-on-one, he'd win, given his inch or so height over hers and his heavier build. Abram would be proud that she finally admitted to herself she was weaker than someone else.

The ferry's sudden jolt announced that they were docking. Good. She would soon be on the road. Heading for the stairs to return to her vehicle, she was abruptly pulled back when Hollander grabbed her arm.

"So you'll stop by the house for coffee, Miss Astrid Lincoln."

"Like I said, it's *Mrs.* Lincoln. And no. I'm going to visit Helena Reese."

He tightened his grip on her arm. She was tempted to test that strength as she would have in former days, but decided to finesse her way out of the obvious threat. She looked around at others on the move.

"I guess everyone is leaving now, Mr. Hollander. I'll be moving now, also."

For a brief second she saw a glint of determination in his eyes. She returned the grimace, so that he would know she wouldn't go with him.

He whispered in her ear, "You really shouldn't wear such fetching polo shirts, *Mrs.* Lincoln. They're far too provocative. I'm only a weak man, after all."

She yanked her arm away. The unexpected jerk pulled him off balance forcing him to take quick steps forward to keep from falling.

"I wear what I want to wear, and you can keep your opinions to yourself, Mr. Hollander. I also go where and when I want to go."

She hastened down the stairs to her Jeep and prepared to drive off the ferry, keeping her eyes straight ahead, not looking around for him.

I'll deal with you another time, Don Hollander, and you won't find me quite so meek then. When you're arrested for flesh trafficking, you won't have anything to grin about.

The gate lowered and as soon as she could, she drove off. Astrid's speed made the bumpy ride to the Reeses' home a bone-rattling experience. In her rear view mirror, she watched the road behind. She kept expecting any moment to see Don Hollander's car following. But he didn't follow and she arrived at the splendid cottage in one piece, relieved to be free of that scavenger.

She barely glanced at the unmoving dark blue water beyond the bluff and the partially restored flower beds, returning to brilliant life. She rang the doorbell on the kitchen veranda and was quickly greeted by Helena herself.

"Come in, Astrid. I'm so glad you came back."

"I'm afraid it will only be until the last ferry this afternoon. Want to pick up my things that I left here. And to see you, of course."

She followed Helena inside where she sat at the kitchen table. They were alone.

"Where is everyone?" she asked.

"They all decided to go with Eddie to Seal Island and see the puffins, since the weather report is for sun and rising temperatures. They can't go onto the island because of the unexploded shells, bombs, and rockets that are strewn over it, left over from navy target practice. But they can see all the many puffins and terns that occupy it for the summer. They're just loading up now. There's time to join them if you want to go."

"No. I have a more serious reason for coming back, Helena."

"And I'll bet I know just what it is. You want to go look for that mysterious light we saw. I looked last night, and it's still there."

Oh dear. Of course that's what Helena would think.

She'll think I'm mad if I tell her about Don Hollander and how I planned to make a citizen's arrest. Maybe I am crazy at that. After all there is no real proof that he's the man behind a human trafficking practice. Dear God, what a fool I am for jumping to that conclusion.

"Well?" Helena said. "Am I right?"

"Ya, of course you are. But maybe I was too hasty to get back here to do that. With your arm in a cast you probably don't feel up to rambling around looking for a light that may not be more than a reflection off something we're not seeing."

Why make an excuse? That light had seemed so important to her before. Now it seemed like a childish thing to pursue. Nothing was going right.

Helena got to her feet.

"It's no problem at all. I feel fine. It was a hairline fracture, the doctor said, and he didn't restrict me in any way. Certainly not from rambling about, as you put it, Astrid. To tell the truth, I'm just as curious about it as you are."

Astrid stood up, too. What the heck? Might as well make the most of it now that she was here.

"Then let's go," she said. "Just as soon as I use the bathroom. It's quite a ride to here from Fairchance."

"Of course. Wouldn't you like a little something to eat and some coffee, too? I should have thought about the long drive, and I'll bet you didn't stop for breakfast."

"No, I didn't. I could use a cup of coffee."

In the bathroom, Astrid looked at herself in the mirror. Her blond hair needed to be trimmed again. Since having it cut, seemed like she needed to spend a lot of time at the hairdresser's to keep it short. Sometimes she wished she still had the long braids, but they were a lot of work and all she had to do now was brush it out.

Don Hollander jumped to mind, and she ceased her self-examination.

"Stupid," she whispered. "Why did you think you could take the law into your own hands and arrest that man? He probably isn't the right man, anyway. There is such a thing as more than one person having the same name. Idiot. Let Abram and Larry and the rest of the law enforcers do the investigating for a change. Just go and have fun."

But his sinister manner still niggled at the back of her mind, and she knew she was only kidding herself. A man with that much ego and desire to be rich could very well be into the illegal stuff. Not that she could fault him about his disdain for island living. She had enough of it to know she would want to go somewhere else and leave the water prison behind.

Helena had juice, coffee and muffins laid out for her when she returned to the kitchen.

"Blueberry muffins. I love them," Astrid said. "I guess I am hungry, at that."

While she enjoyed breakfast, she continued to think about the man she was so sure had masterminded Miriam's abduction. If he hired someone to grab her, could it be that the poor girl was right here on Twilight Isle? However, it begged the question where would he hide her? Where did these terrible men keep innocents like her prisoner? That question needed to be answered and fast, of that she was certain.

CHAPTER 19

Even on a sunny day like this, the salt air felt chilly. Astrid wished she had brought a sweater. Perched on the middle seat of the skiff, she faced Helena who had no trouble handling the small outboard motor with one hand. They skimmed along over the bay ripples, around the island point, heading in the general direction that the light appeared to be positioned each night. Briny drops tapped her face. Maybe it was just that for a few minutes she was actually investigating something that caused Astrid to well up with excitement like she hadn't in all the time she spent on the island this week. This felt right. They would find something important, she was sure of it. Such a flimsy reason to think the light was important, but it just didn't fit the island to have a perpetual, apparently useless light glowing all night. She'd been thinking too much about Don Hollander and what he might be capable of to concentrate on the light, but now the search was on. Now she had something concrete to discover. Now she felt alive.

"You look happy," Helena said. Astrid could barely hear her over the noisy motor.

"Was I smiling?"

Astrid had begun to realize that she often wore her heart on her sleeve, as they say. She had always thought she hid her emotions well. Obviously she didn't.

"It's just the contented look you have."

Helena would notice that. She had the uncanny knack of studying and analyzing people with accuracy.

"I think we may be here," Helena said.

"Here? I don't see anything here."

"Unless I'm very wrong, that light is near the old house that our island scavenger Mort Hudson owns. No one ever goes near it. I think people fear the man. Like I told you, he's the island's scavenger, but I don't think he has ever harmed anyone."

Easing the boat into the cove, Helena steered for the rocky shore. When she could see rocks below the water, she cut the engine and let their momentum carry them as far as it would.

"I need your help now," she said. "With this cast, I can't skull the boat in farther, so maybe you can take an oar and first one side, then the other, push us a little closer where we can get out and pull it in the rest of the way."

Well sure. I can do that. I'm so familiar with boats and long oars and such things.

"Just take one of those oars out of its lock, Astrid."

"Oh ya."

This ought to be good. Be prepared for a dunking.

Nevertheless, she managed, following Helena's directions on moving the boat closer to shore, until she said, "Okay. That's enough. We'll get out here and together we can drag it up on the shore."

Astrid expected to get her old sneakers wet, but when she stepped into the water, she felt what she had not anticipated—it was very cold.

"People actually swim in this ice water?" she asked.

"Don't be chicken," Helena said with a laugh. "Salt water in the north is always cold. If you want bath water, go to Florida."

"Very cute."

With a bit of help from Helena, using her one good hand, Astrid pulled the boat way up over the rocks and attached its rope to a bare tree root above the water line. Two boats rested upside down on the shore above the water line. She'd seen a larger one anchored in deep water, circling its mooring with the motion of waves, at the entrance to the cove.

"How do we get up over the embankment?" Astrid said.

"There's always a pathway somewhere. We just have to find it."

As they walked and searched, Helena asked, "How are they doing in the search for that abducted girl you told me about?"

"I don't think they've made much progress, to tell the truth. You do know about the murder they're also investigating?"

"Yes. Fairchance is getting to be another Chicago with all its crime these days."

"Ouch. I stepped on a sharp stone," Astrid said. "At least I think it was a stone. Ya, lately it seems like our city does have its share of crime."

She was about to tell about Don Hollander when Helena said, "There's the path. See?"

It was barely visible, but beaten down enough to suggest someone had used it a great deal in the past. Helena took the lead and they started the upward climb.

About half way to the top, Astrid said, "Are all islands as high out of the water as this one?"

"Are you out of shape, Astrid? This isn't as bad as ours. It's a real climb over there."

"I'm in great shape. I'll bet I could race you to the top in one breath."

"Well? Let's do it then."

Astrid stood still, looked up at Helena, and saw that she was serious.

"Naw. You'd end up falling and hurting your other wrist, and I might not be able to find you in all this underbrush. What a mess. Shouldn't someone clear the weeds and branches away once in a while?"

"Not if he doesn't want anyone to come calling. And that's my guess."

"Prob'ly right."

They continued the upward climb until they came to an opening at the top, a large clearing surrounded by scrub trees. For a few minutes, they looked around for signs of life.

"I think if we walk over that way," Helena said, pointing across the clearing, "we might come to a road."

Astrid couldn't figure why she thought that, but she tagged along. As they neared the other side, Helena said, "There it is."

"There what is?"

"The cabin or whatever you want to call it. See? Beyond the blackberry bushes. A chimney. Let's go take a look."

Sure. If someone's there, we just pass the time of day and tell them to visit us sometime. Be neighborly.

Helena hurried ahead, but as she drew closer to the fence that surrounded the cabin, she slowed her pace. Astrid wasn't far behind. Her thought was that Helena would likely jump over the fence, at the speed she had been going.

"Now what, camp counselor?" Astrid couldn't help being caustic.

"I don't know. Maybe we can find an opening."

Somehow Astrid had the strange feeling of déjà vu, it was so much like the night the junk yard owner fired shots at her.

"Don't step in that juniper, Helena—you'll get a rash. Maybe we should just chalk it up to having found the site of the night light and let it go at that."

"Oh my goodness. Can it be the fearless Astrid Lincoln talking? Do I hear correctly? Aren't you the one who's always ready for adventure, regardless where it leads?"

"You've been talking to blabbermouths. I've learned..."

"Who's there?"

The loud voice not only interrupted Astrid, it jumped her so badly she grabbed for Helena's arm to steady herself. Helena seemed unfazed.

"Mortimer Hudson. It's Helena Reese and Astrid Lincoln."

"You want something?"

"Not really. We've been seeing a light that seems to come from this way and we thought we'd come over to see if you're all right."

Did he believe her? Would he come out with a shotgun and fire at them? Astrid hadn't felt this uneasy for a long while and she didn't like it.

"Come on, Helena," she whispered. "Let's get out of here."

"No, no. Just wait a minute. It will be all right."

Astrid looked up at a second-floor window. She could swear she saw someone move the yellowed window curtain. Hearing a rusty gate open, she looked to her left and saw that an old man was beckoning to them.

"Come in, Helena. Hain't seen you for an age."

They're old friends. Why didn't she tell me?

"Come on, Astrid. I told you it would be okay."

"Why'd you come that way?" Hudson asked. "A helluva lot easier by road."

Helena laughed.

"I'm not so sure about that, Mort. You don't keep your driveway any better than you keep the path from the shore."

"Guess you got me there. You always was outspoken."

They had walked to the door of the decaying house, and he motioned for them to go ahead inside.

"How's your husband? What's his name?"

"All these years," Helena said, "and you still don't know his name. Shame on you. It's Eddie. And he's just fine. I think he's anxious to go back to France, though."

"Oh yeah. He's the frog you married. You shoulda married me when you had the chance."

"You old goat. Don't call my husband a frog. Besides, you were way too old for me."

"Don't make no matter. Age is only a number. I'm still fit as a fiddle. You're just as handsome a woman as you were fifty years ago, Helena. I clean up pretty good, myself. And I'm still free."

Astrid wondered when, if ever, he cleaned up. Strangely, though, she found that his home was neat and clean.

"You're an ugly old man who takes things from other people. What do you do with all that stuff?"

"I do things with it all. Seems to me I have some of your leftovers, too."

Helena looked bewildered. She tapped her fingers on the table where they had all sat down. She seemed both bold and nervous at the same time. Astrid listened to their back-and-forth with curiosity. She sensed undertones of familiarity that weren't anything like she'd heard from Helena previously.

"Have some coffee, ladies?" he asked.

"Not for me, thank you," Astrid answered. She just wanted to get back to the manse.

"Thanks, but we do need to go back," Helena said.

"What happened to your arm?" he asked.

"I just fell in the storm and got a hairline fracture. Nothing too serious. So it's you who has the light on upstairs, is it?"

"It's me alright. They've been some rowdy teens coming out this way recently. The light's there so's they'll know someone's here. Don't want 'em to get the idea they can just break in for their games."

"Ah. I see. Well, that makes sense. You can always call the constable and have them shooed away if they bother."

"No bother. So far, anyway. Kids that age gotta do what they gotta do. You know?"

Again, Mort gave Helena a meaningful look. Studying his face, Astrid discovered that he wasn't as old as everyone implied. He had a youthful fire in his brown eyes. Could the two of them have been sweethearts at some time? But that was ridiculous. Helena was way out of his class. Still, there might have been a time when he looked a lot different. Older people often looked very different from their youthful image. The patched plaid shirt and grimy jeans meant nothing in particular, except that they didn't get washed very often. But the graying long beard and hair did give him an aged air. Added to all that, his shoulders sloped and he looked undernourished. Yet, he wasn't all shrunk up like an old man. Must be nearly six feet, she decided.

"Why didn't you ever marry?" Helena asked.

"You ask me that? There was only one woman I ever wanted to marry. You should know that."

Helena looked embarrassed by that answer, and quickly stood, pulled herself up to her full height, and held out her hand.

"Good seeing you again, Mortimer."

"You leavin' so soon? I'd like to have you stay a spell. I didn't mean to offend you, you know."

"I know you didn't. It's just that we can't stay. Maybe some other time. We need to get back. You take care of yourself now. You look as if you aren't eating well."

"I eat okay. Not much to keep up for, anyhow."

"Don't talk that way. You see Bella Beaumont a lot, I'm told. Isn't she feeding you?"

"I see her on occasion. She gives me that strawbry pie she's so fond of making. And some other stuff, too. She's a good old gal. Not much of a cook, though. Don't tell her I said that."

Helena laughed and beckoned to Astrid to go ahead of her out the door. At the sound of two thumps overhead, Astrid stopped.

"What's that?" she asked

"Nothing. Just rats. They run all through the walls here," Mort said.

Astrid shuddered. *And you live with them?*

As they walked away, Mort Hudson called, "Don't be a stranger, Helena. Next time I'll tidy myself up a bit before you come over, if you'll let me know."

Again, she laughed, and when they were beyond earshot, she said under her breath, "You old fool. I'm not about to see you again real soon."

They scrambled for the boat, and when they were headed back, Astrid said, "What did he mean that he has some of your leftovers, Helena?"

The answer was slow coming, and Astrid thought it sounded insincere.

"I don't really know. I can't think of anything of ours that has gone missing. I think he's losing it, to tell the truth."

Maybe. But Astrid suspected that it wasn't the truth. Helena had given Mort a definitely fearful, a look that begged for silence.

"Did you believe him that the thumps we heard were rats in the walls?"

"Sure. In an old building like that, it's most likely rats are around, especially near the salt water."

"But I saw the curtain move upstairs when we first got there. You think maybe he's got someone hidden up there? That maybe that's why the light is on all night?"

"Why would he need a light on if there is someone there?"

"I don't know. But I think the two thumps were someone's foot stomping the floor above, like a signal."

"Oh Astrid."

Helena didn't have to say more. Her tone of voice said how moronic the suggestion was.

"Mortimer and I have known each other for many years. He was a good enough person. I have no reason to think that he's evil now, despite his eccentricity."

I guess we see it all differently, then. I think he's hiding someone in that house, and somehow I'm going to find out for sure.

CHAPTER 20

B y the time Astrid got home it was seven o'clock, and she was hungry. Abram came from the den to meet her at the back door. He hugged her close and long. She could swear he was shaking.

"I was worried," he said.

"I'm sorry. Helena and I had a long discussion and I almost missed the last ferry across. Boy, I need food."

"So do I."

He kept his arm around her waist as they headed to the refrigerator.

"You didn't eat yet?"

"No, I waited for you. I was tired anyway and took a nap in my chair."

Really worried.

After frozen dinners were heated, they sat to eat and discuss their day, a habit they started even before they married.

"Anything new at the Demetrie home?" Astrid asked.

She had a lot that she'd like to tell Abram, but she didn't want to get into it just yet.

"Yeah, I'm afraid there is. Once the wife confessed to murdering Nathan, we've been doing a lot of investigating, of course. I still can't quite believe a teenage girl like Tracey has the strength to help lift that dead weight. For that matter, neither could Kay."

"I can't believe it either. Did she say any more about it?"

"We're quite sure someone else must have been involved, but because Kay lawyered up after she confessed, we couldn't ask her anything more."

"Did you find anything else that will help? Kay was what? Jealous?"

"Who knows? From what they both said, the genial mayor had quite a temper and beat up on his wife and kids from time to time. Tracey seemed to have no remorse, any more than her mother did."

"So young, and now Tracey's life is ruined."

"That was a typical dysfunctional family, even with all their wealth."

"It's beyond belief how cruel some people are, Abram. Sickening. I think of poor Miriam being confined somewhere and no way to get help. I just hope…"

She couldn't express her hope. She couldn't say that she hoped Miriam hadn't been forced into prostitution. But she didn't need to say it.

"I know. I hope not, too," Abram said.

Supper finished, they moved from kitchen to the den. Because the evening was cool, Abram started a fire and they snuggled on the sofa. Though they were physically content, mentally they both felt the weight of despair over the growing ugliness that appeared to be spreading in Fairchance. While the mayor's murder had been solved, many questions were left unanswered, and chances of finding Miriam were fading each day.

Abram had long been in thought before he picked up where he left off concerning Miriam.

"I've thought all along that Alice and Oliver Ward know more than they've said. But we've gone over and over it with them, and they insist they were hired to grab the girl and nothing more. They say they were told to drop her off at Lisa's house and that someone would be there to take her when they did. When we asked if someone had been there, they said yes, but they didn't know who the man was. And that's where we get hung up, no matter how we approach them."

"Did they get paid by check or cash?"

"I don't know. No one has said. I wonder if the question was asked."

"Seems like they could describe the man who was waiting for Miriam at the house."

"They say they didn't get a good look at him, which I doubt very much."

"Is there any way you can make a deal with them? A lighter sentence if they cooperate and tell you where Miriam was taken from there, possibly."

Astrid wished she could ask them her questions, but she'd get no cooperation from either Larry or Abram so she'd better not suggest it.

"I'll have to ask Larry if he has made that offer. I almost doubt it. I'm not sure he'd have the authority to do that. This is a kidnap case, for one thing, and that will go to the feds. They'd be the ones to make deals. Maybe if they do, the Wards will open up. It's a good point."

"Odd that they didn't ask for a lawyer, like Mrs. Demetrie did."

"I guess they felt safe enough without one. Probably agreed to what they would say and what they wouldn't way ahead of talking with us. It's really too bad that the mayor was murdered. We were ready to question him about both the abduction and Lisa Smith's murder, but we never did locate him in time to do that. You have to wonder if there was more to his wife's decision to kill him. She wasn't just angry, she was furious when she started talking about him. I wish they had given us the name of the person or persons who helped them."

"That's right. You never found out if Nathan was the killer. Do you have leads at all?"

"Not a one."

"So where do we go from here?" Astrid said. "Are you going to pursue the human trafficker suspect? Maybe look into Don Hollander's background?"

"You won't give up on that, will you? I'll discuss it with Larry. I'll admit it has merit."

"In the meantime."

"In the meantime?"

Mort Hudson had to be hiding something, or someone. She felt certain the thumps she heard were a signal by the person she saw looking out the window. That light wasn't a warning for kids out joy riding. Someone was being held there, she'd bet on it. There was just one way to find out for sure. She had to go back to the island and get into that house again. She'd find a way. But now wouldn't be the best time to speak of it. Tomorrow morning would be soon enough, if she ever did tell Abram what was brewing in her mind.

For now, keep things the way they are and say nothing.

"In the meantime, I think I'll be off to bed," she said. "It has been a long day."

Abram agreed, though he was thinking, *I'll never pass up that option, Sweetheart.*

CHAPTER 21

Tuesday afternoon three printed *Bugle* newspapers were delivered to the editorial office, and each reporter read assigned pages, checking for errors. Finding none of significance, Charlie phoned the press operator and gave him the okay for the full run. They were finished for another week.

"Your story on the mayor's murder was excellent, Astrid. You implied sympathy for Kay Demetrie without editorializing or judging her. We understood that he was a womanizer and an intemperate man. I expect those who knew him well will not be shocked by that disclosure. Tracey sounds like a typical teenager. Tested the parameters of authority once too often, no doubt. Sad thing all around."

Charlie seldom praised a reporter with more than two words— good job, or well done—so she felt like he'd tapped her for knighthood. She almost laughed at that thought.

"Thanks Charlie," she said. "You know, though, that the story isn't finished. At least I'm of the opinion that it's the same story. I could be wrong."

"And that is?"

"The abducted teenager, Miriam Neal. The authorities can't seem to come up with more than who the two are that snatched her."

"You have insight on the case, do you Astrid?"

"Not a great deal. But I'm of the opinion that the answer can be found on Twilight Isle."

Charlie looked as if she'd thrown cold water in his face. He shook his head in disbelief.

"What the hell are you talking about? We just got back from there. Did you uncover something and not tell us about it?"

"Not really. I just know of someone over there who shares the name of a human trafficker, and that he's supposed to be in this area. I don't want to raise false hopes, understand. It may be just coincidence. But I would like the chance to check for more facts. I need to return to the island to do that, like tomorrow, maybe."

Charlie was obviously ready to ask more questions, and Astrid wasn't about to answer anything just yet. She hurried on.

"Will can fill you in about the human trafficker. Will was in Augusta, remember, to unearth information on the subject of human trafficking, especially here in Maine. Okay? Meanwhile, I need to be off. Abram promised to take me to an early dinner and then a show tonight. I need to get home and change pronto."

She gathered her bag and camera while she talked.

"So, I'll see you either late tomorrow or on Thursday morning," she said.

Before he could reply she was out the door racing for her Jeep. Charlie would get Hollander's name from Will. Since she'd said to Charlie where she was going, there was no urgent need to give Abram the same story. She'd simply tell him she would be on assignment most of the next day. He'd never know she was at the island until she returned.

It wasn't as if she wanted to deceive Abram, but he had a habit of being so terribly cautious and she didn't need to have him throw the book at her about staying out of trouble. As if there would be trouble when all she intended to do was wait for Mort

Hudson to leave his house and then go up to the second floor to investigate who was there. Someone *was* there, no question. What a surprise old Mort would get when he came home and found his prisoner gone, assuming there was a prisoner. From the first time she saw the light through the port hole, she just knew something was wrong. Little did she know that an old friend of Helena's was involved in imprisonment, but that was very possible.

It could turn into a bit of an embarrassment, of course. If she did find a prisoner, she'd have to tell Helena about it, and that woman was just as curious as she was. She'd want to know why Astrid didn't get her before searching. But Helena didn't even believe someone was there. She hadn't seen the movement and the shadow behind the curtain, and she believed Mort when he said the noise was made by rats.

Well I don't believe him. I believe he's holding someone in an upstairs room and I want to know who it is and why he's doing that. Since he lied about the noises, I can't see it any other way. I'm surprised Helena believed him. She obviously wasn't still carrying a torch for the old man. Yet, there seemed to be something between them that I just can't figure out. Wonder if she'd tell me if I should ask her straight out. Do I dare do that?

Later, over a special meal at the hotel dining room, she asked Abram if there were any new developments in the murder case. He nodded.

"More detail," he said. "Tracey had a full breakdown in jail before she was bailed out. Larry had taken her to the holding area, and she spilled everything, despite advice from her lawyer. Larry was carrying his little tape recorder and got it all. She painted Nate Demetrie as a monster. He abused her more than her brother, sexually and otherwise physically. I'm not sure how--maybe by following him--she found out where he was going on Wednesday nights, and told her mother.

"Kay brooded about this, and finally convinced herself she could kill him and make it look like suicide, thus avoiding embarrassment about his actions. For some reason she overlooked the fact that an autopsy would be performed, like it or not."

"And she got Tracey to help her."

"That's right. Tracey convinced her boyfriend and another friend to help. They have been picked up already and will face charges, also."

Astrid felt hot and sweaty, almost sick to her stomach, listening to the cold, deliberate action Kay Demetrie had taken.

"What is this world coming to?" she said. "Sometimes I think the islanders have the right idea. Get away from the mad world out there and relax like human beings."

"I expect they have skeletons in their closets, too, Honey."

He looked over at the ornate clock above the bar.

"Oh, oh. Look at the time. We'd better get over to the theater if we want to get good seats."

The movie was basically a romance with some suspense thrown in. Normally, Astrid would have enjoyed the action on the screen, but tonight she was moved to tears in two different scenes. Feeling so emotional had never before been a problem of hers, whether in real life or from fictional stories, but to her complete discomfort she had overwhelming waves of sentiment for apparently very little reason. It made no sense, and she wished it would go away, this nostalgic blubbering.

"You okay, Dear?" Abram asked as the lights came on.

"Ya, of course. Why wouldn't I be?"

"Well, all these tears. I was ready to go get a raincoat."

"Really! I did get into the movie a bit much, I suppose. But I think it was because of our discussion about the murder that touched it off."

"I suppose you're right."

Abram took the wheel going home, and Astrid did not object. However, his stolen glances at her made her feel self-conscious. Why was he so concerned? Did he think she was falling apart, that she had gone off the deep end? What?

She kept her eyes focused straight ahead and her chin up as if she didn't notice his obvious concern, though it was unnerving. After all, women should be allowed a bit of weakness now and then. Just because she was usually stolid didn't mean that she would always be without feelings, and he should damn well learn to live with this exception.

CHAPTER 22

F og shrouded the bay this morning, so much so that Astrid could make out only a gray outline of island from the ferry deck. Like in sound-surround, amplified voices were difficult to pinpoint, lending an eerie feeling of mystery to the setting as people readied to off-load. The scene could have been staged in a London period mystery show. All it lacked was the hollow sound of hoof beats on paving stones and an occasional bobby's whistle.

She strained to see even a few feet ahead while she inched the Jeep down the ramp to the island. She couldn't remember having crossed on this confounded boat when the tide wasn't either low or high. It must be a welcome blessing when it was in-between and you didn't have to worry that the driver ahead of you might lose it and the car come crashing into your vehicle. Astrid wondered how many accidents they had in a year.

Once on *terra firma,* the temptation was to drive directly to Mort Hudson's place and find a good hiding place where she could watch for activity. However, she had passed up coffee again this morning and thought she'd better grab a bite to eat at a local restaurant while waiting for the fog to dissipate. She hadn't told Helena she would come over today. In a way, avoiding Helena now seemed all wrong. The problem was that she might nix the whole idea, come up with a convincing argument that it was a bad plan, speak of Mort's honesty, and wear the day away with trivia like she did before. Astrid wanted none of that. This time she wanted to go back to Fairchance with concrete evidence of foul play going on here.

And what about Don Hollander? He was well hidden from law enforcement here on the island. Couldn't she find a way to flush him out? Oh well, everything would work out, she was sure of it, but had to admit, even with Abram in the Sheriff's Department, that the long arm of the law took its good old time in stretching out for evildoers.

Memory served her well and she drove directly to the little restaurant she had seen on that instructive island tour by hearse. The back parking lot had few vehicles, mostly pick-up trucks. Though the front of the building was neat and painted white like most island business structures, the neglected back wall of blackened brick was lined with tin garbage cans. Astrid had parked and headed afoot to the front of the eatery when she heard her name spoken by a familiar gravelly voice.

"If it isn't the ubiquitous Ms. Lincoln. Good morning."

Such a big word for an islander. He has some education, anyway.

"Good morning, Mr. Hollander."

She had seen him twice before, and both times he was dressed like a leisurely tycoon on holiday, as he was today, all brown and tan color coordinated.

"You mean you're not headed for your friend's for breakfast today?"

"It's a bit early. I'll see her later."

"I can tell you right now that she is not home. You should have called."

"How do you know she's not home?"

"I saw her this morning as she was getting ready to take the ferry across to the mainland."

"I wonder why I didn't see her come off on the other side."

He laughed as if that were a stupid question, and she supposed it was really. Just as she expected, he confirmed her own suspicion.

"People in line to come across seldom notice who leaves the ferry, especially if they're back a way in line, especially in fog."

"I see. Of course."

"Now look, Astrid, we can go in here and have some dishwater that they call coffee, but if you'd like a really good cup and a good doughnut, come with me to my mother's kitchen. Since you can't visit Helena, you can visit with us a spell."

Why did I have to come here and run into this pushy man? And what can I say? He's got me in a corner. Oh well. Maybe I can make this profitable. Maybe I can pry some information out of him when he's relaxed and off guard.

"I hate to put her to the trouble," she said.

"No trouble. She'll probably have a neighbor or two with her. They like her handouts, you know."

"I'm not really looking for a handout, Mr. Hollander."

With that crooked smile and raised eyebrow, he lacked only spats and a long Havana between his fingers to pass for a Chicago gangster of the thirties. Didn't she see him in *Some Like It Hot*?

"Never would have thought it, Astrid Lincoln. You're not an island scavenger. I recognized that when I first met you."

Here she was in faded jeans, one of Abram's old blue shirts with tails hanging below her hips, and the same old sneakers with white socks poking through fuzzy holes. Couldn't look much more like a scavenger.

"So how about it?" he said. "Join me for a really good cup of coffee?"

"Well, okay. I guess I could."

They agreed she'd drive herself and follow him. She recognized the road as the one she'd traveled in the hearse to the lobster pound, though she was too preoccupied with her own thoughts to pay attention to the landmarks along the way. Was this all going to turn out to be a fool's errand again? That question haunted her. There was something on this island, a connection to the kidnap case somehow. In the past her hunches paid off with evil doers being caught.

When she saw the country church, it once again occurred to her how peaceful the area was.

It does seem quiet and idyllic when I look at the church. Ya, and the whole town has a certain charm, too. I wonder if they have a newspaper here.

But that discovery was for another day. At present, they'd arrived at Bella Beaumont's weathered cottage. Her son declared she was a good cook, contrary to what others said. Astrid would soon judge for herself.

Some of the shingles had turned black, but most were gray. The freshly painted white trim and the white picket fence were perfect. Inside, Astrid's sudden fascination with island living was heightened. If someone said a designer had put it together for a fifties homey look, she would not be surprised. The sparkling clean kitchen, with gray and red linoleum flooring, white lace tie-back curtains fluttering lightly at an open window over the white porcelain sink, was right out of an old *Good Housekeeping* magazine.

"How lovely," Astrid said.

A short, heavy-set woman, her silvery hair tucked into a hair net, limped in from another room, possibly a bedroom off the kitchen. Her may-I-speak-now squint and bent posture suggested a humble nature.

"Thank you," she said in the hoarse voice so typical among men and women as they age.

Don put his arm around her shoulders and said, "Ma, I want you to meet Astrid Lincoln. I rescued her at the diner and convinced her to have coffee and doughnuts here instead."

"Glad to meet ya," she said to Astrid. "I made doughnuts early this morning. Just knew someone would be comin' in. Coffee takes just a coupl'a minutes. Sit yourself down here while I get it ready."

"Nice to meet you, too, Mrs. Beaumont."

"You just call me Bella."

"I do hate to put you to trouble," Astrid said, and sat at the table covered by a cracked red oilcloth.

"No trouble atoll. Food's never trouble to me. I love to cook it and, as you can see, I love to eat it."

Despite her limp, she moved like a much younger, lighter woman, and very soon the scent of fresh coffee filled the air. Bella set coffee cups on the table and took fresh doughnuts from the warming oven over the old Magic Chef stove.

As if a school bell had been rung for assembly, the kitchen door opened and Mort Hudson walked in without warning.

"Is that coffee I smell?" he said.

"Just in time, Mort," Bella said. "As always."

"Mort," Don said in greeting.

"Don." Then he saw Astrid. "Well. Mrs. Lincoln, hain't it?"

"Ya. Astrid Lincoln."

She was at a loss what to say to this man whose house she wanted to enter without his knowledge. The four sat around the table for breakfast, and Astrid avoided eye contact with the men, but not Bella. Mort, sitting next to her, glanced her way several times. She pulled as far to her left as possible hoping to avoid the odor of musty clothing over layers of dirt. She sincerely hoped he wasn't like this when Helena was his girlfriend.

At last, Mort said to her, "How is Helena?"

"I think she's okay. I'm just on my way to see her today."

They fell silent. Then Mort spoke again.

"You sailing today, Don?" Mort said.

"I don't think so today."

"I'd appreciate it if you would."

"Not yet."

"He needs to repair my roof before it rains again," Bella said.

Her word was apparently the final word, and the men said no more.

"Are you sightseeing on the island, Astrid?" Bella asked.

"Oh, no. I plan to visit Helena, like I said. Your son saw her take the ferry to the mainland this morning, but I'm sure she'll be back this morning. I can go to her house and wait with her husband."

"Fine people. You're welcome to spend time here, if you like. I don't see many mainlanders these days. Used to. I useta sell fresh produce. Had a stand out front. So when people come over for sightseeing and lobsta feed or fish fry, they'd stop at my stand. I liked that, but I can't do it any more. It's hell to grow old, Astrid. Age saps your strength somethin' wicked. Drains your energy and leaves your joints stiff and sore. I don't recommend it."

"What is it they say?" Astrid said. "It beats the alternative?"

"Don't you believe it. There's days when my back feels like it's broken. My joints feel like they have hot pokers stuck in them. They creak and crack and hurt so bad I feel like callin' Jeremy and tellin' him to bring that hearse o' his and stuffin' me in the coffin. Just take me away to a high bridge somewhere and toss me into the briny. That's how bad it feels. Well, maybe you won't go through this, Astrid. Some don't. I never thought I would."

"Ma," Don said. "I'm sure Astrid doesn't want to hear about your complaints."

"No, of course not," Bella said. "No one ever does. Get old and you're a nobody any more. People look at you as if you should just go home and sit in a rockin' chair. They can't be bothered by old folks like me."

Astrid felt uneasy. The poor woman undoubtedly was suffering. Don probably heard the complaints daily, however.

"It takes getting there, Bella," Mort said, "before anyone understands."

Astrid looked at him in surprise.

"That's right," Bella said. "You and I know, don't we, Mort. We been around the block a few times ourselves. Young people think we was born old like this and just don't understand anything that's going on in the world. I guess we could still teach them a few tricks."

To Astrid's further surprise, Mort laughed.

"I'm not so sure I could teach them as much as you could, Bella, but I still know what direction the sun rises."

They shared a hearty laugh at that.

The pause that followed gave Astrid a chance to speak.

"Your son was right when he told me your cooking is good, Bella," she said.

"Do somethin' enough years and you're bound to get so you can do it well."

Guess I can't argue that.

Don was pushing away from the table when Mort thrust his arm across and grabbed his wrist.

"Let's talk."

"Okay, Mort. Come with me."

The men went into the next room, and Astrid quickly cleared the table for Bella.

"I'll help you wash these," she said.

"No, no. You're a guest. I don't ask guests to wash dishes. I have all day. I'll get to them later, dear. Beats the rocking chair, when I can stand on my feet."

Astrid wanted to hear what was being said in the next room. She could hear only a word now and then until their voices rose in what sounded like an angry exchange.

"I tell you I want her gone."

That sounded like Mort. Astrid stifled a gasp. Could he be talking about the upstairs prisoner?

Bella said loudly, "You still plan to go to the Reeses, Astrid?"

It wouldn't be difficult to think she was trying to outshout the men.

About to reply, Astrid waited to hear Don's reply.

"She isn't going anywhere until I say she is. We'll have another one soon."

"I'm sorry. What was that?" Astrid asked.

"I said, you still going to the Reeses today? You don't want a tour?" Bella yelled.

She *was* trying to cover the other voices.

"I toured the island lately. No I just want to see Helena."

"Like I said, you're welcome to stay with me, if you'd like."

Astrid had to think quickly.

"As a matter of fact," looking at her watch, she said, "I need to get going. I told my husband I'd be home early. I must leave now. Thank you so much, Bella. I'll stop in the next time I'm over this way."

She hurried out the door to her Jeep.

Get out of here fast. Gotta tell someone, but who?

As she drove out of the driveway, her heart beat faster when she saw the men emerge from the kitchen.

CHAPTER 23

In case the men decided to follow, Astrid drove in the direction of the ferry, all the while breathing hard, trying to calm down. When she saw that they weren't behind her, she watched for the east route that would take her to Mort's place. It would mean more miles to cover, but she couldn't take a chance on being seen by Don and Mort. At a boat shop entrance, she parked on the driveway and dialed her mobile phone, hoping to reach Abram. She couldn't think who else to call, but someone needed to know what was going on. At this point it didn't matter what he thought or said about this venture. What mattered most was the life of that person in Mort's house.

"Sherriff's Office."

She recognized the voice.

"David. This is Astrid Lincoln. Put me through to Abram, please."

"Sorry Astrid. He's not here. He didn't know how long he'd be out, but I can take a message."

"No thanks. I'm not where he can reach me."

Should have known. He said he would be talking with Kay's friend today. Now what? Go to Mort's house? Attempt to get upstairs, hoping he'd stay at Bella's for a while? He probably would not stay there long. But whoever he had in his house needed help, and she needed it very soon. Sounded like they were going to take her away by boat. But what did Don mean? Another one? Who would that be?

Human beings are nothing to that man. His personal wealth comes before anything. How does anyone get the notion that they can treat people like cattle? How did it happen that any one person could take on the role of a master over another? Sell someone at auction? Beat someone into submission? It's deplorable. Disgusting. Anyone like that should get a taste of what they inflict on another. Maybe we shouldn't exercise an eye for an eye, but evil should be dealt with, it should suffer—I don't care. I'm glad Abram is fighting for right.

As she drove, she devised a plan for freeing Mort's prisoner. All around Mort's house was nothing but trees and overgrown bushes and brambles. If she could hide the Jeep and approach the place afoot, she could wait in that stuff long enough to see if Mort had gone back another way and got home before she arrived. In fact, she hadn't seen a vehicle at Bella's other than hers and Don's, so he must have gone there by boat. Would he have walked that many miles? Possibly. However, her house was in a valley, very close to the shore. Astrid had looked out a kitchen window and admired the lovely water view. If Mort went by boat, that would mean he'd return the same way, and most likely quicker than the route she took.

Come to think of it, Bella had an ideal place to cast a boat off if they were transporting the woman by water. Mort did ask if Don were sailing today. That answer, though--another one. Another girl, woman, man, boy? Maybe some other cargo. That could be possible, too. Drugs? Counterfeit goods?

Astrid's mind was in overdrive, while she covered the miles to Mort's road. As she approached it, she saw a vehicle at the entrance. Looked like...

"The hearse! What's that doing here?"

Just a pleasant visit to Mort? But Jeremy Barrett had said on the tour that he wouldn't go near the place because of Mort's odor. He had that right. For whatever reason, Jeremy obviously was here, and it meant that she had to make an instant change in plan. He mustn't see her.

"What a snafu this is."

If only she could talk with Abram. Maybe he could have the Harbor Patrol go on the look-out for a speeding craft headed south, she presumed. But would Abram give credence to her supposition? Would he just tell her to stay out of it, to get herself back to Fairchance? Ya. That's what he'd say. Anyone she might talk with would tell her the same. For some reason, no one was inclined to investigate Don Hollander, even though his name was on the list of aliases used by the human trafficking kingpin from Florida. It had to be him.

Well, never mind. I'll take care of it myself. No one wants to help, so I'll find a way. I always do.

That thought also brought to mind the times that she'd taken things into her own hands and sometimes barely escaped alive. Abram cautioned her time and again not to try to solve everything by herself any more, and she wouldn't if he'd just listen to her. The sheriff and his officers could have come here and taken Don in for questioning.

"But no one would listen."

She needed to get away from here before she was seen. She slowly moved the Jeep forward while watching for a place where she could drive off the road and be hidden. Just around a sharp curve she found what she wanted, a grassy area. She knew it could be dangerously wet, but drove in anyway. The ground was solid. Best of all, she found a group of fir trees with an open space that was perfect. She parked, opened her door and stepped into mossy soft grass. She fixed her big black bag over her shoulder, quietly closed the door and locked it. But where would she go from here? Surrounding trees were too dense and dark to try going through them. It appeared she was trapped. She had to go back to the road and find an opening that would lead to the general area of Mort's property.

It's all I can do. I have no choice.

The road was clear when she came out of the woods, but she stayed close to the edge, hoping she would see a vehicle coming before the driver saw her in time to jump into the gutter. She had gone several steps when she heard a car coming. She ran to the woods and flattened herself on her stomach, aware that she was lying on sharp sticks no doubt left by that northeaster. Before it reached the curve, the car engine stopped, but she still couldn't see it.

It must have stopped at Mort's drive. I've got to get over there.

Taking a chance, she ran up to the curve, stopped, and looked before proceeding. In addition to the hearse, Don Hollander's car was now parked near Mort's driveway.

The three of them working together? Incredible. And they're going to take that poor woman somewhere. I've got to stop them somehow. How can I see what's going on? There must be a way to walk down there.

There was! She remembered the gap in the trees she saw when she was with Helena. It was a pathway. So it must come out on this road somewhere. Should she risk walking past the vehicles? The men must all be at the house now. They weren't likely to see her.

Go for it. But hurry. Don't stop for anything.

She ran once again, and almost missed the overgrown path. Not looking left or right, she bolted and crashed onto the path, still running until she came to the open grassy knoll where she and Helena had approached the house from the back. Now she had to be very careful not to be seen by anyone who might be near a window. Crouching low, she hung to the edge where high weeds and bushes hid her from the house. She remembered a dilapidated shed behind the main building, just ahead of her. When she got to it, she took several deep breaths and wiped her wet forehead with a tissue from her bag.

The old boards on the shed walls had shrunk with age, creating gaps through which she would be able to see without being seen. She hoped she wouldn't step through rotted flooring as she pulled at the leaning door. A rusted old lock held it shut. In order to open the door, she needed to lay into it, as Charlie might say. The lock gave way, but not without much noise. She froze. Hearing no one, she stepped inside, still on solid footing. Her eyes quickly focused on the opposite wall where she could watch the house. She took one step.

"Ye-ow!"

She had stepped on a skeleton. Her surprised shout was loud and she feared it may have given her away. Surrounding the bones were old rags that looked like shreds of a uniform. Beside all that was a deflated and torn rubber raft where a long, rusted rifle rested.

"What *is* this? My God, this stuff looks like it's been here for years and years."

Voices. They did hear her. Now what? She looked for a place to go, but the only exit was the way she came in. She was trapped. No need for heroics. Just wait.

She heard Mort say, "It's from the boat shed. Someone's in there. Did you bring a gun, Don?"

"Of course."

Oh good. I'll be shot and left here to rot and wither until I look like this bunch of bones.

She could take that old gun and lunge when the door opened, or she could grab something else and swing away. But in the end, she'd be shot anyway. Might as well face the music.

The door squeaked open and there they were, all three men. Bringing up the rear was Don with handgun drawn.

"What are you doin' here?" Mort said.

"Nothing, really."

"Then why are you in here? What're you lookin' for?"

"I guess I was just curious about this old shed. I'm a born snoop, you know. When I see an old building I want to explore. So that's what I did."

"You came all the way from my mother's to snoop around this old shed?"

Don made a valid point. How could she defend that action? She prayed he had snapped the safety on the handgun he held.

"Well, yes, in a way. I thought that I'd detour and check the shed out before I continued on to Helena's, you see. She expressed an interest in the antique building, too, when we were here the other day and I thought it would be fun to check it out and tell her what's here. And you did say she had left the island. I thought if I could do a little something like this while I'm waiting for her, she might return in the meantime."

"She suspects something, does she?" Don asked.

"Not that I know of." Mort said. "Just a case of two curious women who like old buildings and antiques, I'd say. They did come over to check out the light I leave on upstairs. Helena said they wanted to be sure I was okay."

Jeremy, dressed like he was the day he drove the group to the lobster pound, had been quiet until now.

"Aw, leave her alone," he said. "She's probably telling the truth. Nothing much to do around here, you know. Face it. This *is* an interesting shed."

At that moment his eyes took in the skeleton.

"God a'mighty. Who's that, Mort? I've heard of skeletons in the closet. First time I seen one in a shed."

"Okay. Get out here, Astrid," Don said. "Mort, you take care of locking up here. Jeremy, we'll finish what we started."

Astrid walked into the sunlight, feeling like she'd been jailed for ten years. The dense growth of trees, as well as thick undergrowth, blocked off-shore sea breezes, making the air hot and oppressive. At least she wasn't lying dead or wounded beside a mangle of bones in that shed. If Don had shot and only wounded her, she'd find the conversation rather one-sided in there. No, this was better. All she had to do now was find a way to escape. It wouldn't be easy to get away from these men. Three to one—not the best odds.

Don waved the gun toward the house and pushed Astrid forward.

"You go ahead of me. We need to pick up a package at the house."

A package? It took three men to pick up a package? Or did he mean a live package?

Don helped her along by poking her in the back every few steps, until they reached the door that she and Helena had used on their visit. She wished she could have contacted Helena or Abram. Now no help would be coming and once again she was on her own. What she knew was that the three stooges were not a bit funny. They were dangerous, involved in a horrible scheme, and she had no desire to be part of their game.

Opening the door, Astrid clamped a hand over her mouth to keep from yelling out. Just ahead, tied to a straight chair, was a young—probably teenage—girl making noises but unable to talk with a kerchief tied tightly around her mouth. She wore nothing but pink bra and panties. What had they done to this poor creature? Seeing blood on her legs, Astrid got the ugly picture.

"What are you doing with this girl?" she demanded. "What have you done to her?"

"That, Ms. Lincoln, is not your business," Don said.

"I'm making it my business. You free her right now."

"Or?"

"Or you will soon be locked up for life. You and your cohorts should be shot."

"Those are tough words, indeed. I suppose you'll singlehandedly overpower all three of us at once?"

"You stinking, rotten bastards. What gives you the right to do this to a young girl? Or to anyone? You think you're God? You think someone else's life doesn't matter? What distorted picture do you have of life, anyway?"

"How eloquent you are." Don was laughing at her as if he could play her like a cat with a mouse. "My vision is perfectly good. I like what I see. And I'll tell you for certain that I much prefer you to the inexperience of youth, my dear."

Astrid was frantically thinking of what she'd seen in this place when she was here before. There was no fireplace poker, only kindling wood that she couldn't very well reach down and grab with the mad man so close to her. But the shotgun. In the corner behind the girl. From her position, she couldn't see it. But she remembered seeing it before. Maybe it was still there. On the other hand, maybe he'd moved it. Sheer instinct had taken over her thinking. Death could well be facing her, and she must do something. It wasn't just for herself, it was also for this poor girl.

Out of the corner of her eye, she saw Don's hand reach for her. She moved out of his reach, inching toward the girl.

"You lay a hand on me and…"

"And what? You seem to think some power will strike me down. Sorry. It'll never happen."

His move was quick. He grabbed her arms and held them firmly behind her before she could make her own move. He was strong.

Laughing, Don said to Jeremy, "Now's your chance, Jerry. I'll hold her while you have a go at her."

Jeremy took only a step and stopped.

"No thanks. I don't like this game myself."

"What's the matter with you and Mort? I won't let her go anywhere."

"I mean it, Don. We should leave, now. Take the girl and get out of here."

"I'm not ready to go. If you don't want a turn, I do."

Astrid's years of practice at hand-to-hand combat with her brother and the school bullies reared up in out-of-control angry strength. She went limp all over and pulled out of Don's hands. With one hand against her other fist, she landed an elbow to Don's testes, and effectively interrupted his intention. He bent over, gasping. Before he could talk or move, Astrid was in motion. With a loud roar, she bolted for the corner. The shotgun was still here. She grabbed it up, opened it, and found it loaded. She clicked the barrel back in place and pointed it at Don who'd recovered enough to advance toward her.

"Stand back."

The door opened and Mort came in. He stopped short when he saw Astrid with the gun.

"That's loaded," he said.

"Sure it is. You all know what two barrels of double oughts can do. If any of you move toward me, I'll pull both triggers and watch the pieces of flesh fly. I'm not afraid of killing you. Given the circumstances, I'd be justified."

All the while she was talking, Astrid used her left hand to pull the kerchief off the teen's head.

"You able to walk?" she asked.

The girl nodded.

"What's your name?"

"Miriam."

"Thank God."

The rope was only loosely tied and Astrid had no trouble loosening it to free her.

"Go get dressed quick-like, but don't get fancy. We're getting out of here."

Miriam dashed out of the room and up the stairs, remarkably agile considering how much pain she must be in, Astrid thought.

Still holding the shotgun, Astrid continued, using her most powerful, commanding tone.

"I'd like nothing better than to just shoot you all. Miriam and I are leaving here through that door. Move away from it, all of you. Over to the other side of the room. Make no false moves."

Miriam was quick to dress. She came running down the stairs still buttoning her blouse. Astrid kept her eyes on the men, holding the shotgun in both hands, ready to shoot without a second thought if one should rush at her.

"Stay close behind me, Miriam. We're walking out. Come on."

She saw Don's movement toward the door.

"You want to lose a particular part for good, Don, or your whole life in one shot?"

He stopped and went back.

She could hear Miriam wheezing while they moved. At the door, Astrid told her to open it and run up the roadway. When she got a good head start, Astrid gave one more warning before dashing out herself, shotgun still in hand.

"If anyone comes through that door within the next fifteen minutes, you're a dead man. I guarantee that."

CHAPTER 24

Astrid led Miriam to the Jeep, got in herself and drove it out of the woods, heading away from the direction she had come. It took only seconds for her to learn that she'd made a mistake. The road came to a dead end at the top of a cliff, where she was stopped by a high cable fence with a huge sign, STOP.

"No, no! I forgot about the ravine. What a dumb ass I can be sometimes." She looked over at Miriam and saw that she was horrified.

"Don't worry. I'll get us out of here."

She drove around the wide turn-space and backtracked until they came around that blind curve. There, parked across the road, was the black hearse, with the three men waiting for her to return. Don had his handgun pointed at her. More determined than ever to get away from these men, Astrid saw an open space around the right of the hearse. She was sure it was large enough for the Jeep to get through, but it also looked soggy. She could see standing water where she would have to drive.

"Buckle up, Miriam, and press back in the seat as hard as you can."

She slowed down, and just when the men began to saunter in her direction, no doubt thinking she would have to stop, she slammed the accelerator to the floor. The luxury Jeep swerved back and forth. She saw the men run to the front of the hearse. Don raised his gun, but he was too late. She had maneuvered around the blockade okay, but when she felt the wheels sink beneath her, she had to fight panic.

"Come on, baby, you can do it."

She slammed into reverse, then gunned it forward again. This time the wheels got traction on solid road. They were away before Don fired the first shot. The men would need a few minutes to get themselves on the road, and she knew she could outdistance them now. Astrid never had a light foot when it came to driving, but the Jeep's speed had not been tested so thoroughly as it was this day. She took the most direct route into town, where an inquiry at the gas station led her to the constable's office, "Over there in the fire house."

Keeping Miriam with her, she found a fireman near the open fire house doors. He directed her to a side door inside. On entering, she found a small, unadorned room with an oak desk at the side by an open window. At the desk sat a broad-shouldered man smoking a cigar. He had a deeply tanned, leathery face, and bushy dark hair. His dark green uniform was embroidered simply Constable in yellow. On his cluttered desk top, a sign announced Constable Trask. As he looked his visitors up and down, his smile turned to a perplexed frown, and he ground his cigar stub to smoldering stubble in a glass ashtray.

"I need help quickly," Astrid said.

"I thought as much. Take a chair."

Astrid pulled a straight-back chair closer to his desk, and Miriam sat by the wall on a similar chair.

He said, "You are…?"

"Astrid Lincoln. I'm from Fairchance and my husband is the sheriff's detective there. This is Miriam Neal. She was abducted a few days ago on a country road outside Fairchance and has been held prisoner here on the island."

"I read the flyer that she was missing. She's been a prisoner here, you say?"

"That's right. By Mort Hudson. And…"

"Wait a minute," he interrupted. "Mort Hudson? The island's petty thief? You say he abducted this girl? I knew he was light-fingered, but stealing a girl?"

"No, no. He didn't. Don Hollander had her abducted, and he brought her here. He and Hudson work with Jeremy Barrett. I'm pretty sure they are all part of a much larger gang that deals in human trafficking. I can fill you in with details later. For now, it's imperative that we get word to the sheriff and my husband that I have Miriam with me and that the men they want are still on the island. But I think they plan to make a quick getaway in a boat."

"This doesn't make sense," Trask said. "A gang operating here on Twilight Isle?"

His expression clearly said he thought she was a nut case who should be locked up herself. How could she convince him?

"No, I know it doesn't make sense, Mr. Trask. Trask. Are you related to the woman who runs the lobster pound?"

"She's my aunt by marriage."

"Listen to me, please. I'm a friend of Helena and Eddie Reese. As you can see, if you'll look at her legs, Miriam here has been terribly abused by these three men, Hollander, Barrett, and Hudson."

Trask looked down at Miriam's legs, and she pulled a shorts leg up higher so he could see the blood.

"They did this to you?" he asked.

"Yes. Please, she's telling the truth. They were going to send me somewhere, but I don't know where or what was going to happen."

"How did they get you here?"

"I was put aboard a boat in Twin Ports and taken here to a house. It's where Don Hollander lives. At night he took me to Mort Hudson's, and I've been kept upstairs with a light on twenty-four hours every day. It was Don Hollander who hurt me."

"Good god-a-mighty."

He picked up the old dial phone.

"You have a telephone number, Mrs. Lincoln?"

She gave him the sheriff's number and he dialed. Soon he was talking to Larry Knight. If he'd been before a judge and got a life sentence, Trask couldn't look more worried.

"Okay. Yes sir, I'll do that."

He handed the phone to Astrid.

"He wants to talk with you."

Almost limp with relief, Astrid listened while Larry told her that he would have a Coast Guard boat there pronto to take them to Twin Ports where an ambulance would be waiting.

"Good. I'm not sure where the men were going, but it sounded to me like they planned to go by boat. However, if they took that hearse, that was made over for taxi service, they might try using the ferry. It could be more efficient for them on the mainland as a get-away vehicle. There's a casket in the back of that hearse, supposedly for luggage. Everyone thinks it's a real joke."

"Good thinking, Astrid. I'll have the ferry watched. The constable will take you to where the Coast Guard will pick you up. We'll have an ambulance take her to the hospital. You want to talk with Abram?"

"Ya, if he's there."

"He is. Hold on."

Abram's voice was shaky.

"Astrid. What's going on? You're at the island?"

"I'm okay, Abram. Ya. I'm with the constable on the island."

She heard Larry's voice in the background.

"Hold on," Abram said.

When he came back, he said, "Larry just briefed me. I told you not to get into trouble."

Oh, boy, he was angry.

"Well, it's a long story, Honey."

"No doubt. Would it have been so difficult for you to tell me where you were going this morning?"

"I know. I should have told you, but I was so sure they had a prisoner in that house. I was right. I could hardly believe it when she said she's Miriam. She's with me and she needs medical attention, Abram. Larry said he'll have a Coast Guard boat pick us up."

Sometimes she could kick herself for this tendency to jump in with both feet. But she did feel coming here was the thing to do when she started the day.

"Abram, Miriam's parents have to be told. She needs them. Find out, please, what hospital they'll take her to, and have the parents go there. Will you do that?"

"Of course. You say you're all right? Didn't get tortured or shot at?"

She would tell him about the confrontation later. For the moment, he seemed calmer. He might be hurt that she didn't confide in him, but he wouldn't be angry with her.

"I'm just fine. All whole, no scratches. I love you, Abram, and I'll be there soon."

"Yeah, okay. Stay out of trouble in the meantime, okay?"

Hanging up, Astrid said to Miriam, "There will be an ambulance waiting when we get to Twin Ports. They'll take you to the hospital for attention. You need to be examined after the ordeal you've been through. They'll do what needs to be done, and you'll be all well before you know it."

"Are you coming with me, please?"

It was a pathetic plea that went straight to Astrid's heart. The girl had stood up so well through it all, but now she was trembling and close to tears.

"Of course I'll stay with you until your parents get there. You'll be given good care. Most of all, you must be brave."

"I'll be okay if you're with me."

Astrid would never tell Miriam, but she had already decided to pay all medical bills for the family. At times, her grandfather's fortune was a real blessing. The best part of it was that few knew she had a large inheritance. She and Abram had agreed not to make that the important issue of their marriage, and they both worked as if they needed to. Astrid would have it no other way. Occasionally she found a good cause to support, like this one.

Before leaving Constable Trask's office, Astrid dialed Helena's private number, not really expecting an answer. To her surprise, she was home and answered on the first ring.

"Helena, it's Astrid. I have something important to tell you," she started.

"I know. Poor Mort did have a prisoner, just like you thought. I apologize for doubting your instinct, my dear."

"You know? How?"

"Apparently the other two men left him alone when they took off. He called me and told me the whole story. I wasn't entirely honest with you, Astrid. You see, there was a time when I considered marrying him. He was a good-looking, very nice young man. I thought he'd make something of himself even though he came from a poor family. It was my father who put a stop to that intention. When I met Eddie, I left all that behind. Mort made his living fishing before he had a heart episode and had to give it up. The scavenger activity that he carried on after that brought him enough income, I guess, to provide food. At least that's what everyone thought. There is so much more to tell you. I can't do it on the phone like this."

"No. I have to leave with Miriam. Look, come to my home Sunday, will you? Come before noon. That will give us plenty of time to talk."

"I will. And, Astrid, you are every bit as brave as your friends say you are."

The conversation left Astrid with more questions than answers. She looked forward to hearing answers. For now, she and Miriam followed the constable to the dock where they waited for the arrival of the Coast Guard.

CHAPTER 25

For the rest of the week both Astrid and Abram worked long hours, he with continuing investigations into the two murders, and she, along with Will, investigating and writing features about the ever-increasing revelations concerning human trafficking activities.

By Sunday, they were ready for a change of pace and the opportunity to relax with friends. Helena and Eddie arrived at eleven, and Astrid had lunch ready and waiting in the refrigerator. The hot day was ideal for shrimp salad rolls with iced tea. Later they could make their own sundaes.

Once they settled in the living room, Helena asked the first question.

"Mort said you were in his old boat shed, Astrid. What did you find in there?"

Odd question. Why would Helena be interested in the contents of that shed?

"I had almost forgotten, we've been so busy," Astrid said, "I'm sorry I forgot to tell you about this, Abram. I stepped on old bones. I think it was the skeleton of a soldier because there were pieces of a uniform around the floor. There was also a rusted long gun.

And an old helmet. Do you know anything about it, Helena? Did Mort say?"

"As a matter of fact, I know all about it."

Helena reached for Eddie's hand next to hers.

"Eddie and I agreed that we'd tell you about it, since you'd likely have an investigation into the matter. You have our permission to do with it what you will. You see, Eddie is German."

"German," Astrid said. "I thought you were French, Eddie."

"She'll tell you."

Helena continued.

"Very near the close of the Second World War, Eddie was a German seaman. He saw so much cruelty in that war, especially as Nazis *cleansed* their occupied countries, that he decided he wanted to become an American citizen and get away from a country he no longer knew."

Eddie took over.

"I had to jump ship in order to do that. Sometimes we do exceptional things, hoping for the best outcome but prepared for the worst. I was prepared to be imprisoned if I was caught. It was the most difficult thing I ever did in my life. Right from the start, I knew my action was rash, but I had an overpowering desire to be free of that darkness and try to forget the horrors of the war."

Astrid and Abram exchanged bewildered glances. The turn of this conversation was not what they'd expected.

"Our boat surfaced and began its journey back the night I planned to take the plunge. I dove into the bay and found that the water was very rough due to a sudden squall. Worse than that, it was ice water."

"I can believe that," Astrid said.

"At one point, I thought I couldn't swim any more and I would just let myself drown. But then I saw the island I had chosen for my escape, and somehow I managed to get there."

Astrid interrupted with, "That's why you were so concerned that night Helena drove off in the northeaster."

"Sure. She knew as well as I did that anything can happen in a storm like that. But let me tell you, you cannot even imagine the feeling of utter hopelessness that came over me when I realized I was entirely alone, sick from the exertion of getting to the island, and frightened that someone would come along and shoot me. If it hadn't been for this wonderful woman, I'd have died, I'm certain of it."

He held her hand to his lips.

"Oh my," Astrid said.

Helena continued the explanation.

"Along the coast we had been warned of a German submarine combing the waters. There was much speculation that the war in Europe would end very soon…that was in early May of 1945… so most everyone had pretty much regarded the talk of a U-boat on our coast as active imaginations at work. But you couldn't disregard the possibility that there might be such a boat and should they come ashore, there might be a confrontation with one or more Germans, maybe even in our homes. I was at the island for a brief respite from my work and planned to leave within three more days.

"Well, that night of May first, I was alone and felt nervous for some reason. I kept turning off my light and going to the window to look down over the back yard. The storm was finally clearing away and the moon peeked through clouds now and then. When I saw a man half crawling toward the house, I got the small handgun Father had given me and taught me to use. So when Eddie came into the house, I was waiting behind a door I left ajar enough to see him. He came in quietly through the kitchen door, and started to look for food in the cupboards. That's when I turned my flashlight on him with the intention of blinding him momentarily. I saw this thin but handsome blond German, with wide, wide blue eyes, so wet and cold he was shaking. I must admit, I was at a loss what to do with him, but I just could not kill him."

Astrid leaned forward.

"What *did* you do, Helena?"

"Well, because I lived in Germany in my early years, I could speak German."

"You're German, too?"

What an incredible turn of events. Both of them German, she thought.

"No, I'm French. My father was an architect. He went to work for the German government in the twenties, not knowing, of course, what they were up to. When he did hear the rumors of pending war, he intended to pack us all up, and go back to France. In about 1938, he sent me on ahead to the care of my aunt, and he and my mother stayed to pack the household items. I never saw them again. I don't even know for sure if they were executed as traitors. That's what I suspect.

"My aunt and her husband adopted me. They never said my parents were dead, but I concluded that they were when they became my parents legally. When it appeared Paris would soon be invaded, we moved to the United States where my aunt, rather my adoptive mother, had an estate on Long Island. It had taken me no time to learn French. You may have guessed that this man, whom I soon learned to call Father, was Marvin's grandfather. Marvin's father, who became my brother, was older than me when I was adopted by his parents, so we weren't very close. I guess no one thought it was necessary for Marvin to know that I was adopted. I never told him. He was young when I began going abroad as an interpreter."

Abram was no less fascinated than Astrid and wondered aloud, "So when did you have an interest in this Mort guy?"

"I guess I was about 20, and spent most of the summer on the island. We met at a church ice cream social, and afterward he called on me a few times. I guess he thought if he asked, I'd marry him. When I said no, he gave it up."

Astrid shook her head.

"I'm still back where you spoke German, though you were French, and now Eddie speaks with a French accent, but you don't."

"Very simple," Helena said. "I couldn't keep Eddie at Twilight Isle, needless to say. So I drove him off the island on the last ferry the next day. I told him not to say a word. But as it was, he didn't need to worry about talking. I was working as an interpreter in Washington. Few people really knew me well then. No one spoke to me on the ferry. He and I sat in the car going across, and from there I drove us to Long Island where he could stay in my mother's family home. I couldn't take him to Washington, so he remained on Long Island as a gardener until I was no longer needed in Washington. I hired a close friend to teach him English. All of this had to be kept secret, of course, and only a few knew about Eddie. Even my parents knew nothing about him. Mother lived with Father in Fairchance by then. You know, Father started that print shop and newspaper that my brother inherited, and when he died, Marvin inherited both."

"Marvin *had* both," Astrid corrected, "but he sold the newspaper to Dee before they were married."

"Right. Well, Paris came back to life after the war ended, and we decided to go there, get married, and remain while he learned French and better English. I have an ear for languages and learn them easily. While I studied Chinese, Eddie found French to his liking. So even though he speaks English well, he maintains the French accent. Most people think I went to Paris and married a Frenchman."

They all sat quietly for a few moments before Helena laughed and looked at her husband.

"Every time I think of that fateful night when you came to my back door, I have to laugh."

She looked at the others and explained.

"He could speak very little English—like I said, just a smattering—and when he learned that I spoke German, he explained how he planned to defect and become an American. At some point when he thought to introduce himself, he told me that his name was Eddie Smith."

"A German named Eddie Smith," Astrid repeated.

All four laughed heartily.

Eddie said, "My real name was Karl Ludwig. But she liked the name Eddie and I kept it after that. When we were married, we had to decide what last name to use."

"I thought it would be a good idea for us to take the name I was born with-- Reese," Helena said.

"I think we got off course," Eddie said. "You wanted to know about that skeleton you found at Mort's house."

"Yes," Helena said. "I should finish that part of it. We told you how Eddie came into my life. Well, it didn't go exactly smoothly. Seems he was seen going into the water from the U-boat, and a lifeboat was sent after him. I got Eddie something to eat after he cleaned up and changed into some of my father's clothes upstairs. We talked a good deal at the table and suddenly a German sailor burst through the door with the intention of taking Eddie back to the boat.

"I had put the little gun in the pocket of my robe. The intruder pointed his rifle at me and Eddie tried to defend me. He didn't know that I was able to use a gun, of course, but he found out. I simply shot the German through my pocket. We were sure he was dead, so I told Eddie to come upstairs with me in order to get a small mattress that we could haul him on and put him into my car. When we came back down, the body was gone. We never knew what happened to him. We checked the beach the next morning and couldn't find the boat or any sign of him. Eddie said he must have just been stunned, and when he regained consciousness, went back to the boat and left the island. But I have always had the feeling that I killed him.

"All these years, and finally I found out that I didn't kill him after all. Mort told me that he was doing his usual shore patrol when he saw the man stumble down over the stairs. By the time the German got to his boat, Mort was at the edge of the water. He raised his rifle and shot him. That time, he was dead."

Astrid said, "And he never told you?"

"Never, until now. I lived with guilt that I may have killed someone. I couldn't be sure that he didn't die after maybe dragging himself out of the house and to his boat. Of course, it would have been called justifiable, since we were still at war.

"Mort deflated the man's boat, and put body and deflated boat into his boat, ran them around the island to his own place and left the body in that shed. He didn't worry that anyone would go in there. He didn't want me to get into trouble, so that's why he did it."

"Remarkable," Abram said.

"How come Mort called to tell you all that?" Abram asked.

"Conscience. He knew he would be picked up by authorities very soon. He was repentant that he'd let himself get taken in by Don and held Miriam at his house, but the money he was to receive blinded him, I guess. Then he thought of that skeleton, and wanted to make it right with me. Mort is basically a good man. I do hope he will be given some leniency."

"I don't know," Abram said. "Kidnapping is a federal offense, and he did hold her against her will for several days."

They all murmured their understanding.

"We have a couple of questions ourselves," Eddie said. "Have you found Don Hollander yet? Your story said authorities picked up the other two, but not him."

Abram rose from his chair and went to the polished brick fireplace, where he rested an arm on the mantel.

"We did get him. At first, we thought he managed to leave the state. But not so. With Mort's willingness to tell all he knew, we learned that he was still at his mother's house. Bella Beaumont had him hidden under a tarp covering his big boat. Mort said he was still with Bella and told us just where to search. He didn't get a chance to hide the second time. Bella is also charged, since she harbored a criminal."

"Oh, I'm sorry to hear that," Astrid said.

"And that couple who kidnapped the girl?" Helena asked.

"When they were told that we had all the players in this operation, they told what they knew—details about Lisa Smith and how she planned her own get-away in the mayor's boat. Demetrie wouldn't have killed her if she hadn't refused to take part in the trafficking scheme any longer. None of them in this area were in it long, only since Hollander arrived back at his home on the island."

"Abram," Astrid said, "did you ever find out what the code in that red book meant?"

"Uh huh. The Holts knew about it. Seems they were quite friendly with Lisa Smith. She had told them that she was keeping tabs on when Don Hollander and Nathan Demetrie were planning to sell someone. She devised that code. It's really quite simple. For instance, 1GB – 6-5 -92 means one girl by boat on June 5, 1992. And after each G she wrote either B or H, boat or hearse. We found four of those entries, so apparently they shipped out four teenage girls, mostly by boat."

"I guess the mayor played a major role in that scheme, but Don Hollander was the ring leader," Astrid said.

"That's right."

"How is Miriam?" Helena said.

"She's doing very well," Astrid replied. "Considering what she went through. I hope she'll be able to rise above it, but it's not easy. You know, Dee is wonderful at counseling. She ran a summer rehabilitation camp for alcoholics for ten years. She must have been very successful. I took her with me to visit Miriam. She just has the knack of talking with her that sets the girl at ease. I'm sure Dee will keep up her visits until Miriam can face society with self-confidence again. Right now she doesn't want to testify against those monsters, but by the time they are taken into court, she should be up for it. She has a sweet family. Her younger sister and her mother cried when they saw her in the hospital the first time. I think her father wasn't far from tears himself."

"What a complex, criminal web of evil it has all been," Helena said. "The murders and the kidnapping. And to think that Don Hollander was responsible for most of it."

"I would correct that," Abram said, "and say that he was responsible for all of it. If he hadn't brought the proposition of human trafficking to the two men on the island, Miriam would never have been abducted, Lisa Smith would not have been murdered, and probably the mayor would still be alive."

"How did the mayor figure in all of this?" Eddie said.

"He became acquainted with Hollander, who convinced him he could become a multi-millionaire in the trafficking of teens. Of course, he was already a good customer of Lisa Smith's, so he convinced her to help, only she got religion, as they say, and told him she was finished with the unthinkable act of selling innocent teens. We know the outcome of that--he killed her and moved the body to her own house. Mayor Demetrie's daughter Tracey followed him one night to Lisa Smith's.

"Even though Tracey did not like her mother much, she told her about Nathan's rendezvous. That enraged Kay so much that she killed her husband and threatened to kill Tracey if she didn't help her. What a mess. A lot of innocence lost in this one."

When questions appeared to be exhausted, Astrid sat back and sighed.

"Well. I guess we can summarize all of this by saying it's over. Now, maybe we can have some peace and quiet for a spell. I know I'm ready for a break."

At that, a chorus of laughter filled the room.

"I'm afraid we all know you too well, my dear," Abram said. "If there's a hint of trouble, you'll be in the middle of it."

*****

Long after their guests left, Astrid and Abram sat at the kitchen table to have coffee and a snack before retiring for the night. They went over all that had been revealed this afternoon before they decided to call it a day.

"I don't know about you," Abram said, "but I'm tired. Feel like I've been awake for a week."

"Me too," Astrid said. "But there's something that I think we should deal with first."

"What's that?"

"You remember I asked if you wanted children?"

"Ye-es." Abam's drawn-out inflection hinted at the dawn of understanding.

"Well, I'm really glad you said you do."

"Because?"

"Because we're going to have one in about six months."

Abram said nothing for so long that Astrid feared he might not be happy with that declaration. When he stood up, however, he erased her doubt.

Pumping his arms over his head, he yelled, "Yes! Yes! Yes!"

"I guess you like the idea, then?"

"Astrid, my love, right now I couldn't get higher if I guzzled a quart of Johnny Walker straight down. Come here, and let me show you just how happy I am."

Printed in the United States
By Bookmasters